THE MISSING CHUMS

Something is amiss in Bayport, the Hardy boys' home town. First, there is trouble in Shantytown, then a strange black craft tries to ram Joe and Frank's boat, the *Sleuth*. That night the local bank is robbed. And later that same night the young detectives' pals, Chet Morton and Biff Hooper, mysteriously disappear after a masquerade party.

Are the events related? And do they emanate from Shantytown—or from Hermit Island, an isolated land mass inhabited for many years by a strange recluse? Is it significant that both the missing boys and the bank robbers wore masquerade masks? Or is it more important that Chet was wearing a costume identical to Frank's?

One by one, Frank and Joe tackle the clues, hardly daring to think what might have happened to their missing friends. But it is not until the two brothers confront the kidnapers that the overall pattern begins to emerge. The kidnapers ruthlessly plan to force Frank and Joe's famous detective father into choosing between justice and his sons!

How the Hardy boys use all their courage and skill to outwit the criminals provides an exciting climax to one of the most baffling mysteries the young detectives have ever encountered.

"I hate to think what *that* costume means,
if it's a signal," Joe said

THE HARDY BOYS

BY FRANKLIN W. DIXON

THE MISSING CHUMS

Grosset & Dunlap
An Imprint of Penguin Random House

GROSSET & DUNLAP
Penguin Young Readers Group
An Imprint of Penguin Random House LLC

Penguin supports copyright. Copyright fuels creativity, encourages diverse voices, promotes free speech, and creates a vibrant culture. Thank you for buying an authorized edition of this book and for complying with copyright laws by not reproducing, scanning, or distributing any part of it in any form without permission. You are supporting writers and allowing Penguin to continue to publish books for every reader.

Cover illustration by Ryan Brinkerhoff.
Cover design by Mallory Grigg.

ISBN 978-0-448-48955-1   10 9 8 7 6 5 4 3 2 1

CONTENTS

CHAPTER I

Exciting Assignment

"Joe, how soon will you be ready to roll?" Frank Hardy burst into the garage where his brother was working on a sleek, black-and-silver motorcycle.

"Right now, if this machine kicks over," Joe replied, putting down a wrench. "But what's the rush? We're not going to meet Chet and Biff for two hours."

Joe looked up quizzically at his brother.

"Chief Collig phoned," Frank said. "You'll never believe it, but he has a case for us."

"You're sure he didn't mean Dad?" Joe asked. Fenton Hardy was a widely known private investigator. His sons had learned from him about sleuthing, and acquired a great deal of skill.

"Positive. He said he wanted the detective's sons this time—and right away."

"Wow!" Joe exclaimed happily. "What a

break! Summer vacation and a mystery to solve!" He swung into the saddle and kicked down hard on the starter. A roar filled the garage and he grinned in satisfaction.

Dark-haired, eighteen-year-old Frank had jumped onto an identical motorcycle, standing beside that of his blond brother, who was a year younger. The two machines roared out into the hot morning sunlight. Ten minutes later the boys arrived at police headquarters in downtown Bayport.

They were greeted by the desk sergeant. "Hello Frank—Joe!" He waved them toward the chief's office. "He's waiting for you."

"Come in, boys," boomed Chief Collig through the open door. He was a vigorous, middle-aged man with iron-gray hair. "I'll get right to the point. There's something funny going on in the squatter colony at the end of the bay."

"You mean Shantytown?" Joe asked, referring to a settlement of shacks on the ocean shore north of Bayport. The odd community was composed mostly of men who had seasonal or temporary jobs—and some who did not work at all.

Chief Collig nodded. "The men there seem to be in an ugly mood—violence and fighting at night. The charitable landowner who permits them to stay there wants us to investigate, but it'll have to be an undercover job because those drifters recognize the police."

"And that's where we come in?" Frank guessed.

"Yes. I want you to put on old clothes, muss your hair, and hang around Shantytown for a while. See if you can discover what's been stirring up the group. Will you do it?"

"Will we!" Joe exclaimed without hesitation. He turned to Frank and added, "Chet and Biff aren't due at the boathouse for an hour. Let's take a look at Shantytown."

"Thanks, boys. Be careful," Chief Collig said as they hurried from the office. Outside, Frank and Joe mounted their motorcycles and rode through the downtown traffic to the Bayport waterfront.

Leaving the big commercial piers behind, they took the Shore Road, past a section of private docks to where the brothers kept their trim speedboat, the *Sleuth*. Driving on, the Hardys followed the road along the curve of the left bank of the bay to the mouth of the harbor. Here they turned north and continued parallel with the ocean.

Soon they saw a jumble of board shanties on the wide beach ahead. Some were nothing more than open lean-tos, but others had glass windows and stovepipes. Pieces of ragged clothing fluttered from ropes in the breeze. Smoke curled up lazily from a small fire around which three men lay, watching the steam from a black pot which hung on a tripod above the flames.

The boys parked a distance away and observed

them intently. "Looks peaceful," Joe commented.

"A lot of them must be away at work," Frank remarked. "Remember, the trouble comes at night, when they're all here together."

After studying the quiet scene for a few more minutes, Frank said, "We'll come back later."

The brothers turned their motorcycles around and headed toward the outskirts of Bayport, where the many private docks lay. Brightly painted cabin craft and sailboats with slender masts rode at mooring floats.

Seeing a yellow jalopy parked in front of the Hardy boathouse, Joe remarked, "Chet's here."

Frank and Joe parked their motorcycles beside his car, named the Queen. A broad-shouldered, good-looking boy stepped through the small side door of the boathouse. He held a key, one of the duplicates the Hardys had given to their close friends.

"Hi, Biff!" Frank greeted him. "Where's Chet?"

Biff Hooper answered in an unnaturally loud voice and winked at them. "Why—uh—he'll see you soon."

"What's up?" Joe whispered.

Biff merely shrugged and kept on grinning. The Hardys knew some joke was in the making!

Frank asked in a low tone, "Have you opened the bay door yet?"

Biff nodded. "And unmoored the *Sleuth*."

Frank raised his voice and continued talking with Biff, at the same time motioning to his brother to tiptoe to the boat door.

Joe chuckled, took a bamboo pole from against the boathouse, and picked his way across the catwalk to the front. He peered in, then upward.

Jammed between the rafters and the ceiling was plump Chet Morton! He was looking the other way, toward the small door.

Silently Joe unmoored the *Sleuth,* and using the pole, pulled the craft halfway out of the boathouse, leaving a clear surface of water beneath Chet. Then Joe playfully jabbed at his friend with the bamboo pole.

"Yow!" Chet bellowed. There followed a great splash, and a geyser of water drenched the inside of the boathouse, as the chubby boy went under. A second later he popped to the surface, just as Frank and Biff ran in.

"Why, Chet, what are you doing in the water?" Frank asked, pretending astonishment.

"As if you didn't know! Where's Joe?"

"Right here, Chet," he said.

"All right, you turned the tables," Chet sputtered good-naturedly as they hauled him out of the water. "I was going to scare you. Biff, did you give me away?"

"Of course not." Biff laughed. "If I'd known it was a swimming party, I'd have worn my trunks!"

Chet grinned and began peeling off his wet

shirt. "Good thing I wore *my* trunks under my clothes," he said.

In a few minutes his wet garments were drying in the stern of the *Sleuth* while the powerful craft, with Joe at the wheel, cut smoothly through the waters of Barmet Bay. The boys munched on sandwiches, which Chet had brought along.

"Say, how about a camping trip, fellows?" Biff suggested. "We could go to some of the islands along the coast."

"This boat would hold plenty of provisions," Chet chimed in.

"We can explore Hermit Island," Biff went on. "I heard that the old man who owns it lives there all alone."

"Afraid we can't, fellows," Frank answered. "We have a new case." Quickly he told them about it.

Biff whistled appreciatively but Chet groaned. "Ever since you solved *The Tower Treasure* mystery, our lives haven't been the same."

With a twinkle in his eyes, Biff said, "Chet was hoping that would be your first and only case."

"The last one you took on was nearly the death of me," Chet grumbled. He was referring to his adventures with the Hardys while solving *The Secret of the Old Mill.* "From here on," he declared, "just leave me out of any mysteries!"

His friends laughed, knowing how Chet hated to be left out of anything.

"Yow!" Chet bellowed

"Too late," Joe told him. "We're heading for Shantytown to take another look-see."

By now the speedy craft was far out on the broad bay. The water had grown choppy and was turning from green to steely gray. In the distance the boys watched a cluster of white sails skimming before the breeze.

"A race," Biff observed.

"Hey! Look out!" Frank cried sharply.

A black hull, parting the water in white sheets at its prow, was bearing straight down on the *Sleuth's* rear on the portside.

Frank shouted and waved frantically at the oncoming boat. "Cut her, Joe!"

Still the strange craft roared along toward the boys. At the last moment it came about, throwing a heavy bank of water aboard the *Sleuth*. For a moment the two boats sped forward, gunwale to gunwale. The name *Black Cat* was on the prow of the strange boat.

"Not so close!" Frank shouted angrily. The pilot ignored the warning. He was a swarthy man with black hair combed straight back. At his side sat a huge man with a bald head.

Calling on the *Sleuth's* reserve of power, Joe shot the craft forward, veering to the right. The boys looked back with satisfaction as the black boat dropped behind.

Facing forward again, Joe caught his breath in

horror. Directly ahead loomed the great white sails of the racers, bearing down on them swiftly. He cut the wheel frantically to the left.

"Hang on!" he yelled. "We're going to hit!"

CHAPTER II

An Evening of Mystery

INSTANTLY Frank grabbed the steering wheel held by his brother. He twisted it violently and pulled out the throttle at the same time.

For a moment the *Sleuth* banked hard and balanced on her side, while the huge tilting sails hovered overhead!

One—two—three—four—dark sailboat hulls sliced safely across the speedboat's boiling wake as she shot outward into the bay.

"Wow! That last one only missed us by a foot!" Biff exclaimed.

"Oh, boy, let's not do that again!" Chet said shakily.

"You okay, Joe?" Frank asked as he slid back to his side of the boat.

"Yes, thanks to you! Where did the *Black Cat* go?"

"There she is!" Biff shouted.

Looking around, the brothers saw that the other speedboat had veered in plenty of time to run easily before the sail craft. The big, bald man was pointing to the boys and laughing.

"Bank her again, Joe!" Frank cried angrily. "We're going after those men!"

"I can't!" Joe shouted back over the roar of the engine. "She won't respond to the wheel."

Already a quarter of a mile of open water separated the two boats. Helpless, the four friends watched the black craft race away.

Meanwhile, the *Sleuth* shot ahead at full speed, her handsome prow lifted clear of the water.

"Do something!" Chet cried. "We'll run aground!"

"No, we won't," said Frank, who had noticed the curving white swath of their wake. "We're going in circles."

The *Sleuth*, her steering mechanism disabled by Frank's emergency turn, was clearly completing a wide circuit.

"We might as well save gas," Joe said, throttling down. "One thing's sure. We won't make Shantytown today."

Glumly the four sat still while the distant shores seemed to rotate around them. To the east, where the bay opened toward the sea, a grayish mist lay over the black water.

"Look at that fogbank," Biff said. "I hope we're not stuck here when it rolls in. It would be mighty hard for anybody to find us."

"I don't think that pea soup will move in before dark," Frank said, but there was a note of concern in his voice.

"We're supposed to go to Callie's costume party tonight," Chet reminded the others, "so we'd better get out of this mess soon!"

Suddenly the boys' attention was diverted by the high whine of a motorboat plowing toward them across the water.

"More trouble?" Chet muttered.

"Trouble, nothing!" Joe exclaimed. "It's the *Napoli!* Hi, Tony!"

The four companions waved wildly at their friend and in a few minutes a yellow speedboat idled up alongside the *Sleuth*.

"Thought it was you," said dark-haired Tony Prito from behind the wheel.

"Why are you fellows running in circles?" asked Jerry Gilroy, who sat beside Tony.

"Our steering's fouled up," Joe reported briefly. "Give us a tow, will you, Tony? I'll tell you about it on the way in. Chet, let's have that line back there!"

Taking a coil of rope from the stout boy, Joe scrambled onto the prow of the *Sleuth*. He secured the line at the bow, passed it to Jerry in the *Napoli,* and then climbed into Tony's boat himself. While the *Sleuth* bobbed along toward Bayport in the wake of the *Napoli,* Joe told the newcomers of the near collision.

Twenty minutes later the six friends stood together on the dock of the Bayport boatyard while a mechanic examined the *Sleuth.*

"You think the fellow tried to sideswipe you on purpose?" Tony Prito asked.

"Yes, I do," Frank said. "They saw us clearly and heard us shouting, but they came straight at us, anyhow."

"Maybe something went wrong with their boat," Tony suggested. "It could have been an accident."

"Accident!" Chet Morton snorted. "You should have seen the look on the bald man's face after we skinned past that last sailboat. They were out to get us all right."

"But why?" Jerry inquired. "Did you ever see them before?"

"Never!" Joe stated positively. "But I certainly hope we see them again!"

"We'll report this to the Coast Guard," Frank said. "They may want to talk to those two men."

Just then the young mechanic joined the group. "You have a damaged rudder," he reported to the Hardys. "I've fixed it temporarily, but you'll need a new part to do the job right. It'll take a day or two for me to get it. Bring your boat back then."

"I'll follow while you take the *Sleuth* to your boathouse," Tony volunteered. "Then we can all go to the Coast Guard station in the *Napoli*."

After the Hardys' craft had been safely moored in their boathouse, Tony headed the *Napoli* out into the bay. He turned and followed the shoreline to the long jetties where the freighters were docked.

Soon the *Napoli* passed under the gray bow of a big cutter moored at the Coast Guard pier. Tony made his boat fast, and the six boys climbed up a steel ladder onto the dock. They entered the small, neat station office, which had a short-wave tower on its roof.

The officer on duty rose from his desk. "Hello, Frank—Joe—fellows," he greeted them. The personnel at the Bayport station knew the Hardys well. More than once they had cooperated with the boys and their father on cases.

"Hello, Lieutenant Parker," Frank said gravely. "We want to report a near collision caused by a powerboat named the *Black Cat*. Can you tell us who owns her?"

Quickly Frank gave an account of the incident while the officer took notes. Then a seaman who had been listening brought over a heavy ledger, which he spread open on the desk.

Lieutenant Parker ran his finger down the list of names and licenses of speedboats on the bay. "Nothing here, fellows," he announced, looking up. "She must have come in from an outside port. Have you noticed a boat like that in the last week or so, Thompson?"

The seaman thought for a moment. "No, sir," he answered. "But there's been a big regatta going on up the coast for a couple of days. She may have run down from there."

"We'll go up and find her!" Joe put in eagerly. "What town is it?"

"Northport."

"Not so fast," Frank said. "Don't forget our other business, Joe."

"You win," Joe replied with a rueful grin, "but I hate to see—"

"We'll have our patrol boats keep a lookout for the craft," the officer promised. "If we find it, I'll call you."

It was late afternoon when the *Napoli* plowed through rough water on her return to the Hardy boathouse. To seaward, the wall of mist had mounted higher and moved in closer, so that now it seemed almost at the harbor's mouth.

"The fog's coming in fast," Jerry remarked as Frank, Joe, Chet, and Biff disembarked. The Hardys thanked Tony for his help.

"That's okay," he replied. "It's getting late. We'd all better go home and get ready for Callie's party."

"Don't forget your costume," Joe called as the *Napoli* churned away. He turned to Chet and

Biff. "How about you, fellows? Are you all set for the masquerade?"

"I am!" The fat boy chuckled in anticipation. "Wait'll you see what I'm going to wear!"

Biff grinned. "Even you detectives won't know us."

"We just have time to pick up our costumes from Mr. French before he closes," Frank noted.

A few minutes later there was a clatter as Chet backed his jalopy onto Shore Road and he and Biff drove off.

The Hardys kicked their motorcycles into life and started toward town. When they reached Bayport's main street most of the stores were closing.

"We're in luck!" Frank declared as he parked in front of the costume store. "It's still open. Mr. French has a couple of customers in there!"

The boys hurried toward the door. Through the wide shopwindow they could see the tall, spare proprietor, with thinning blond hair and a small graying mustache. He was talking earnestly to two men whose backs were turned. None of them noticed the boys.

As Frank pushed open the door, Mr. French stopped speaking. The taller of the strangers raised his voice and said in an ugly tone:

"Well, you're in this *now,* French, and don't you forget it!"

CHAPTER III

Faces in the Fog

THE door clicked shut behind the Hardys and the speaker whirled. He was a slight man with gray hair, pale skin, and small dark eyes. His brow was furrowed in a deep scowl, but in a flash he assumed a genial smile.

"Hello there. You startled me. I didn't hear you come in."

His companion was short and darkly tanned, with almost white-blond hair. He gave a little laugh and nodded. Even Mr. French assumed a thin smile, though his eyes had a worried and uncertain look.

"Sorry to interrupt," Frank said, "but we've come for our costumes."

"You didn't interrupt anything, fellows," the blond man assured them. "Just a little standing joke we have with Mr. French. We've known him for years. But every time we come to town he says he won't go out for a good time with us. So we have to get tough with him. Isn't that right, French?"

The shopkeeper smiled weakly and stammered, "Yes . . . of course . . . that's right." Nervously he fingered a small costume box on the counter in front of him. Then, to Frank and Joe's surprise, he added, "These are the sons of the famous detective, Fenton Hardy. Excuse me, I'll get their costumes." He hurried into the back room.

Both strangers looked steadily at the boys a few moments before the gray-haired man spoke up. "I recollect that your father was once an eminent member of the New York City police force."

"That's right," Frank replied.

"And haven't you young lads received attention in the public eye for your own exploits?"

Frank and Joe looked uncomfortable at the flattery. Before they could answer, Mr. French returned with two cardboard boxes. He opened one and took out a hairy-skinned gorilla costume. Its ferocious head was a rubber mask to fit over Frank's head.

"Going to a party, eh?" asked the white-haired man.

"Where will the festivities be held?" inquired the other.

"At a friend's house," Frank replied evasively.

"Of course." The man gave him a hard look.

Then, taking the small costume box from the counter, he said, "Well, we wish you a pleasant evening, young gentlemen. Good night, Mr. French!"

With a cheery wave of the hand, the gray-haired stranger went out the door, followed by his short companion. As they walked past the window, the Hardys looked them over carefully.

"Is my suit ready too, Mr. French?" Joe asked, after the men had passed from sight.

"Yes—the magician's outfit. Here it is."

The shopkeeper opened the other box and held up a rubber mask with a long nose, sinister slanting eyes, black mustache, and goatee. Joe looked at it for a moment with approval, then returned it to the box.

"We'll bring the costumes back tomorrow," he promised, and the brothers left the shop.

"Something queer was going on in there," Frank said as they placed the boxes in the carriers of their motorcycles.

"I think that gray-haired fellow was threatening Mr. French," Joe declared. "Old friends, my foot! Did you notice how Mr. French tried to cover it up?"

"Maybe he didn't dare do anything else," Frank suggested. "He looked scared to me. Let's ask him about it tomorrow. He might be in some kind of trouble."

"Okay," his brother agreed as they mounted

their motorcycles. "But we're going to be busy on that Shantytown case."

Minutes later, the two motorcycles swung into the Hardy driveway. "Say, I have an idea!" Joe said, as the boys left the garage together. "Let's put on our masks and give Mother and Aunt Gertrude a surprise."

Frank chuckled. "I'll ask what's new at the zoo."

The brothers pulled the false faces over their heads and went to the front door. As Joe pressed the doorbell, chimes sounded within. The boys thrust their faces forward.

After a pause the door was opened by a tall, thin woman whose angular frame froze momentarily to stiff attention. Her mouth opened and closed twice. On the third try her voice succeeded.

"You're repulsive! Go away!" she cried and slammed the door.

The brothers burst into laughter. "Poor Aunt Gertrude!" said Frank. "It isn't often we can fool Dad's smart sister!"

The door opened again, revealing a handsome man with the build of an athlete. "What's going —?" Then he began to laugh. "Okay, you nuts. Come in." Frank and Joe ripped off the masks and walked into the living room.

"You!" Aunt Gertrude exclaimed.

"We're sorry, Auntie," Frank said. "Joe and I didn't mean to scare you so badly. These are masks we're wearing to a masquerade party tonight."

Mrs. Hardy, their slim, attractive mother, smiled. "They *are* realistic. No wonder you were frightened, Gertrude!"

When Miss Hardy was mollified, the family sat down to a delicious chicken dinner. Between mouthfuls, Frank and Joe told about the near collision on the bay and of their conference with Chief Collig.

"It could be an important case," Mr. Hardy said. "Good luck."

But his sister had other ideas. "I don't like it in the least," she declared. "Two young boys among those roughnecks in Shantytown!"

"Frank and Joe know how to take care of themselves," Mrs. Hardy said. "Don't worry."

"I'm warning you," Aunt Gertrude said to the boys. "One of these days something terrible will happen to you! Just remember I told you so."

Seeing the teasing twinkle in Joe's eye, Mrs. Hardy spoke up quickly before he could reply. "Where's the big party tonight?"

"Callie Shaw's," Joe answered. "Frank can't wait to see her."

"Oh-ho!" his father teased. "And I suppose you, Joe, won't look for Iola Morton as soon as you get there?"

The brothers grinned at the mention of the two girls they liked best.

"Callie and Iola are giving the party together," Frank explained. "That reminds me, Joe. We're supposed to pick up the ice cream!"

A short time later, as Frank and Joe stepped from the house, they noted the gray, leaden sky overhead.

"Looks as if that fogbank has moved in from the bay," Joe commented. "It'll be thick downtown."

After stowing their costumes in the carrier behind Frank's motorcycle, the two boys set off for the center of Bayport. White wisps of fog swirled in the glare of their headlights and almost blotted out traffic. Both riders slowed to a cautious pace.

At last the boys maneuvered to a stop in Milton Place just off Main Street. Through the fog and gathering dusk, vague lights could be seen in the big brick building on the opposite corner.

"They're working overtime at the bank," Joe pointed out and grinned. "Counting the extra money they took in during evening hours."

The brothers walked around the corner onto Main Street and entered a soda shop. Minutes later they emerged, each carrying a two-gallon drum of ice cream packed in dry ice.

"Wow! This is cold!" said Joe, as they turned into the alley.

Frank and Joe placed the cylinders in Joe's carrier. "Now for the party!" Frank grinned.

Suddenly they heard a harsh grating noise and

looked down the narrow street to see a heavy side door swing open in the bank building. There was a clatter of footsteps on concrete, and four men hurried from inside, carrying white sacks. Their faces looked like those of hideous beasts!

For an instant the Hardys stood paralyzed with surprise until Frank cried out, "It's a bank robbery!"

In a split second the men dived into a waiting sedan. Its powerful engine roared. As the getaway car moved down Milton Place through the mist, a bank custodian raced out and fired his revolver at one of the car's tires, but missed.

"Let's tail 'em, Joe!" cried Frank, leaping onto his motorcycle.

CHAPTER IV

A Daring Getaway

FRANK and Joe gunned their motors and took off down the narrow street after the bank robbers. Tires screamed as pursuers and pursued careened through the fog-filled streets toward the Bayport waterfront district. Through the haze, the boys could see the red taillights of the bank robbers' car.

"They're heading for the docks!" Joe shouted as he recognized the long, dark shapes of warehouses on both sides of the murky street.

The fleeing car shot out onto a wide pier, lighted at intervals by yellow fog lamps. Ahead, a four-foot wire fence barred motorists from the pier's end.

· Brakes squealed sharply. In the amber glow, the Hardys saw the four doors of the thieves' car pop open at once. Five dark-coated figures piled out and jumped the fence.

The Hardys' motorcycles screeched to a halt

behind the empty getaway car. "Stop!" shouted
Frank, leaping off. "Help! Police!"

A clatter of footsteps sounded far out on the
jetty. Frank and Joe vaulted the fence and
sprinted in pursuit.

The sound of heavy breathing told them they
were nearing their quarry. But as the boys
reached the end of the long pier a powerful boat
engine suddenly roared to life.

There was a churning of water, a whiff of gasoline smoke, and the sound of men jumping into
the boat. Then the craft gained headway in the
darkness of the bay.

"We can still stop them!" Frank exclaimed.
"The Coast Guard station's on the next pier.
Come on, Joe!"

The boys dashed back, cleared the barrier, and
ran past their motorcycles. Suddenly they heard
shouts and footfalls approaching along the pier.

Omph! With stunning impact, Joe collided
head-on with a running man.

"Look out!" Frank shouted as strong arms
grasped him.

"Halt!" a voice ordered. "We've got you!" A
whistle pierced the air. For a moment all was
confusion. "Now—what's going on here?" demanded the authoritative voice.

"Let us go! Bank robbery! We need the Coast
Guard!" Frank said, gasping.

"We *are* the Coast Guard," replied the voice,

and a flashlight shone through the fog. "Why, it's the Hardy boys. Release them, men," said Lieutenant Parker.

"We heard somebody shouting for police," he added. "What's this about bank robbers?"

After Frank had explained, the officer said, "I'll dispatch a cutter after the bandits right away." Lieutenant Parker and his men raced off.

Moments later, a police car sped onto the pier, its siren wailing and red top light blinking. It stopped and three uniformed men leaped out.

"There's the car!" cried one of the men. Even in the heavy fog, Frank and Joe recognized him as the bank guard who had fired the shots after the fleeing robbers. "The crooks got into that car, and then these motorcycles raced off with them."

Suddenly he spotted Frank and Joe. "Those are the bodyguards who rode the motorcycles. Grab 'em!"

A grim-faced policeman, gun in hand, ordered Frank and Joe to come forward. Apparently he and the officer with him were new members of Bayport's police department, for the boys had never seen them before.

"All right, what do you two have to say about this?" the patrolman demanded. Again Frank told what had happened.

The policeman turned to the guard. "Is that the way it was?"

"Yes—no—" the man stammered, highly excited. "The robbers had on hats and pea jackets. And they wore horrible-looking masks."

"Look at this!" called the second policeman, who had been examining the car and the motorcycles. He came over, holding up the gorilla face in one hand and the magician mask in the other. "These were in the carrier of that cycle. I guess we've got two members of the gang."

"Now wait a minute!" Joe began, but the wail of a siren cut him short.

Two more police cars arrived and heavily armed men poured from both cruisers.

The first officer to reach the group was Chief Collig. "We got your radio call!" he told the policemen briefly. "Any sign of the bank robbers?"

"Two of them—right here!" the man replied. He jerked a thumb at the Hardys.

Joe stepped forward quickly into the beam of yellow fog light. "Hello, Chief!"

"Frank! Joe!" Collig cried out in astonishment. "How did you get here?" He faced the startled rookies and said, "These boys are all right."

"But," one of the men protested, "according to the bank guard the thieves wore masks. And we found these on one of the cycles." He handed Chief Collig the false faces.

"You'll find four gallons of ice cream, too, Chief," Frank put in. "We're on our way to Callie Shaw's masquerade party."

The chief laughed heartily, but quickly became serious again. "Any suspicion of these boys is nonsense. Now, what about the bank robbers?"

Quickly Frank told him all that had happened.

"I guess it was too foggy to see their getaway boat," the chief said gloomily.

"That's right," Joe answered, "but from the sound of it, I'd say it was an open speedboat, with a powerful inboard motor."

There was the ringing of bells and the deep rumble of engines from the next pier.

"The Coast Guard is taking the cutter," Frank said. "But even their powerful searchlights won't pierce through this pea soup."

"Their best bet is to crisscross the bay and perhaps close in on the robbers," Joe added.

"And for that a little boat is as good as a big one," Frank said excitedly. "Joe, do you think the *Sleuth* is in good enough shape to take out?"

"It's worth a try," his brother assented.

Chief Collig nodded approvingly. "The more boats we send out, the better our chances," he said. "I'll dispatch the police cruiser, too."

Frank and Joe swung onto their motorcycles and roared off the pier and along the Shore Road toward their boathouse as fast as they dared in the heavy fog.

Guessing they were near the private docks, the boys pulled off the road and parked. Each took a flashlight from the carrier of his motorcycle.

After a short walk they found their boathouse. Joe reached the small door and took out his key. He gave a cry.

"The lock's broken off!"

"What!" Frank exclaimed.

He swung the door open and beamed his flashlight inside the building.

The *Sleuth* was gone!

CHAPTER V

Dancing Gorillas

FOR A moment Frank and Joe stared at the empty boathouse unbelievingly. "I'll bet the bank robbers stole the *Sleuth!*" Joe exploded.

"If they did," Frank said with a grim smile, "they may be surprised. That rudder is only temporarily repaired. It won't last long."

"Let's go after them!" Joe urged. "We'll call Tony to bring the *Napoli.*"

"Okay," Frank said. "He'll be at Callie's now."

The Hardys hurried to their motorcycles and headed back toward town. When they reached the piers, they stopped at a public telephone booth outside a warehouse. Joe dialed the call and returned after a short conversation.

"Tony will meet us at the Coast Guard station," he reported to Frank. "Come on!"

When the Hardys walked in they found that Chief Collig had turned the place into a temporary headquarters. He was questioning three bank tellers who had been brought there at the chief's request. One teller was giving his account:

"The four men must have hidden in another part of the bank. Just after we closed tonight, the robbers rushed into the main room together. Three came to our cages and forced us at gun point to put all the money into their sacks, while the fourth went to the side door. Then they warned us to keep still, and backed out the door. Our vault custodian fired after their car, but had no luck."

"Can you describe just one of the gang?" Collig asked wearily. "Any one that sticks in your mind? Was he short or tall? Fat or skinny?"

"I already told you," the man said doggedly. "They were all the same size."

"But blast it, man, that's impossible!" the chief exploded. "I don't have four identically built men on my whole force!"

"They were all the same size," the teller repeated, growing sullen. "They wore masks."

Shaking his head, Chief Collig turned from the teller. His eyes fell on Frank and Joe. "Back so soon?" he asked, surprised.

Frank told him about the stolen *Sleuth*. "The bank robbers used a speedboat for their getaway," Joe added. "It might have been ours."

"Has the cutter had any luck on the bay?" Frank asked.

"Nothing yet," the radio operator spoke up. "They've been calling in every ten minutes."

While Joe reported the theft of their boat to a Coast Guardman, Frank asked whether any clues had been found in the thieves' car.

"Not even a fingerprint," was Chief Collig's answer. "We checked on the vehicle, of course. It had been stolen in Northport."

Just then Tony Prito entered the crowded station, exclaiming, "It looks like a police convention outside, with all those prowl cars!"

"Hi, Tony," Joe greeted him.

"Thanks for getting here so fast!" Frank said.

The three boys left the station at once, ran across the pier, and scrambled down a ladder into the *Napoli*. Tony started his motor, switched on his running lights, and throttled cautiously into the bay.

The surface of the water was smooth and the air was warm. The fog, however, was thicker than ever. Tony tried his spotlight but even this did not penetrate the murk for any great distance.

"Suppose we zigzag along shore about half a mile out," Joe suggested. "The Coast Guard will cover the middle of the bay."

The *Napoli* moved steadily through the night. The boys could see nothing.

"We need our ears for this job," Frank said finally. "Shut her off a minute, Tony."

The steady purr of the motor ceased and the

craft drifted noiselessly. Far to seaward, outside the harbor's mouth, a deep-voiced foghorn rasped its warning at regular intervals.

"Nothing," Joe muttered disgustedly. "Start her again, Tony!"

"Wait!" Frank ordered. "There—another boat!"

"I don't hear it!" Tony whispered.

"It's very high-pitched—just a tingle. Turn her out into the bay, Tony. Run full throttle until I say stop."

The *Napoli* shot forward, roaring through the fog.

"Stop!" Frank cried out.

Again came the sudden, hushed silence. Only the wake of the *Napoli* washed audibly behind them. But now all three boys heard the sound of a boat engine.

"You were right," Joe whispered. "I think it *is* the *Sleuth*. Listen!"

The high-pitched whine drew slowly closer, then gradually receded. Soon it approached again.

"She's going in circles!" Joe chortled gleefully. "Head toward her, Tony."

"Sure. But which way?"

"To the right," Joe said promptly.

"Straight ahead!" Frank countered.

Tony started his engine and headed midway between the two directions. He drove steadily forward until Joe signaled to cut it again.

The other craft was very near them and over the motor's purr they could hear angry voices.

"It won't *work!*" one cried out. "Try it yourself!" Another shouted, "Move over, then!"

Frank, Joe, and Tony listened, grinning, while the men argued about the disabled boat. Suddenly the *Sleuth's* motor was silent.

"They're drifting away," Frank said quietly.

Although Tony followed in the direction he thought the other boat was taking, the voices grew faint. Desperately Tony opened his throttle wide, then shut off the motor again to listen. The voices had ceased.

"The men must have heard us," Joe whispered. "They probably know they're being chased."

For a time the eerie pursuit continued, but at last Frank said, "It's no use. They could have drifted a mile away by now."

"Or they could be five feet from us," Joe whispered. "We'll never find them in this fog."

"Besides, we're low on gas," Tony added, and turned the *Napoli* toward Bayport.

"Joe and I will come to the party later," Frank told Tony. "I think Dad would like to hear our account of the bank robbery."

After dropping Frank and Joe at the Coast Guard pier, Tony returned his boat to its mooring and went back to Callie's house. Meanwhile, the brothers, dejected, cycled home. Opening the front door, they found their father in the hall taking his hat from the rack. Mr. Hardy stopped short.

"Tell me what you know about the bank holdup," he said crisply. His sons stared in surprise.

Then Frank grinned. "I guess Chief Collig told you about us, didn't he?"

"Yes," replied Mr. Hardy. "He just phoned to ask my help. I'm on my way downtown. Brief me quickly."

The detective listened with keen interest while his sons poured out the story of the robbery and the missing *Sleuth.*

"One thing is odd," Frank added when they had finished. "The tellers swear the thieves were all the same size and build."

Fenton Hardy smiled. "That's not so strange."

"You mean the men *were* identical in size?" Frank asked.

"Not at all," their father answered. "But a large mask will make a person's body seem smaller. A tiny face mask can make him look bigger."

"So the robbers used the masks to disguise their builds as well as their faces," said Frank.

"Exactly," his father answered. "It sounds like a very clever gang."

At that moment Aunt Gertrude came into the living room. "Fenton," she said, her voice sharp with disapproval, "there was a special news bulletin on the radio just now saying that you've taken on the Bayport bank robbery case."

"So I have," Mr. Hardy replied mildly, though the boys knew he was an expert at this. "At least to help the local authorities," he added.

"But why do they announce it?" his sister asked tartly. "The bank robbers may hear it, and who knows what those dangerous men might do to make you drop the case!"

"Don't worry, Gertrude," Mr. Hardy replied kindly. "I'll be careful. Thanks for the information, boys," he added, and hurried off.

Aunt Gertrude eyed Frank and Joe suspiciously. "What are you two going to do now?" she demanded.

"Nothing dangerous, Auntie," Joe assured her. "We're just going to Callie's party." Satisfied, Miss Hardy watched the boys depart.

"Aunt Gertrude's right, you know," Frank remarked as they walked to their motorcycles in the drive. "It's too bad about that radio bulletin. Dad is safer if he works under cover."

A short ride brought Frank and Joe to the Shaw house. They parked their motorcycles beside the garage and quickly put on their costumes. Carrying the two containers of ice cream, the gorilla and the magician walked to the door, where they were admitted by a smiling Mrs. Shaw.

"Hello, boys. Come right in! I'll put the ice cream away."

When the Hardys entered the big living room they were hailed by a camel with four human legs, Spaceman Prito, and many other fantastic figures.

Pretty, brown-haired Callie was dressed as a fairy princess, and slim, vivacious Iola as a page boy. The two girls hurried forward to greet the late arrivals.

"Tony told us about the robbers and the chase," Callie said.

"We're glad you got here!" Iola added warmly.

A fierce pirate strode up to them. "I'm Black-beard Biff Hooper," he announced. "How'd you like to walk the plank?"

Before Frank could answer, there was a ferocious roar behind him and a hand clamped down on his shoulder. He whirled to find himself face to face with another gorilla!

"Told you I'd surprise you!" came Chet Morton's voice. "Come on, Gargantua! Let's dance!"

The two hairy creatures joined hands and waltzed around the room to the music of the record player. They pirouetted, leaped in the air, and did somersaults. The other guests watched, shrieking with laughter. Panting, Chet yanked off his tight-fitting gorilla face.

"Oops!" he exclaimed ruefully. "I tore it."

Frank examined the rubber mask. "Too bad,"

he said with a grin. "You'll have to wear your own face from now on."

Later, as the guests ate, they listened, fascinated, to the Hardys' account of their adventure. Finally, about midnight, everyone began to leave.

As Frank and Joe were saying good night to the girls, Chet came over to them. "Biff, Tony, Jerry, and I have decided to go camping tomorrow. We're using Mr. Hooper's boat. Sorry you fellows can't come."

"We'll make it next time," Joe promised.

Iola said to Chet, "You can go on home and drop Biff at his house. I'm staying overnight here."

"Okay, Sis."

Frank and Joe departed, and soon after returning home, they were sound asleep. Two hours later the ringing of the telephone jarred the silence of the Hardy home. Frank awoke and picked up the extension phone.

"Hello."

"Frank?" The speaker was Mrs. Morton. "Is Chet there? He hasn't come home yet!"

"No, he isn't here," Frank answered. "He probably went to Biff's."

"I'll try the Hoopers," Mrs. Morton said. "Sorry to have awakened you."

As Frank replaced the telephone, he glanced at his wrist watch. It was two o'clock.

"Funny Chet didn't phone his folks," he thought.

A second later the phone jangled again and he picked it up. "Frank Hardy speaking."

"This is Mrs. Hooper," said a worried voice. "Is Biff with you?"

Frank sat straight up in bed. "I'm sorry, he isn't here," he replied. "I'll call some of our friends and see what I can find out."

Biff's mother gratefully accepted the offer. "Oh, thank you. I'm so worried about him."

As Frank put down the phone, Joe mumbled sleepily, "What's the matter?"

"Matter? It looks as if plenty's the matter. Wake up! Chet and Biff are missing!"

CHAPTER VI

A Perilous Slide

STARTLED by the news, Joe sat bolt upright in bed. "Chet and Biff gone?"

"They vanished after the party."

"Who was that on the telephone?" suddenly asked a deep voice. In the doorway stood Fenton Hardy in a robe.

Quickly Frank told his father and Joe about the calls from Mrs. Morton and Mrs. Hooper. Mr. Hardy promptly dialed police headquarters, and identified himself to the desk sergeant.

"Have any accidents been reported since midnight?" he inquired. As he listened, the lines of his forehead relaxed.

"None," he reported to Frank and Joe. Then the detective explained the situation to the officer, who promised that the police would look for Chet and Biff.

After putting down the phone, Mr. Hardy

asked his sons, "Is there any place the boys are likely to have gone?"

"They were planning to go camping early this morning," Joe recollected, "stopping at different islands along the coast. Maybe they decided to go tonight instead."

"I doubt it—in this fog," Frank objected. "And not without telling anyone." Nevertheless, he dialed the Hooper home to make sure.

"Oh, no," Biff's mother replied to Frank's question. "Mr. Hooper carries the boathouse key with him. If Biff and Chet had wanted to leave earlier, they would have had to get it from him."

Frank tried not to show his mounting alarm. Hoping he sounded cheerful, he said, "We'll keep looking for the boys." After saying good-by, he turned to Joe and his father. "This is serious. I hate to disturb Callie, but I'll *have* to now." He dialed her number. Callie herself answered sleepily.

"Sorry to bother you so late," Frank said. "But will you do me a favor? Peek out the window and see if Chet's jalopy is there. It was parked under the street light."

After a short pause he turned to Joe and his father. "It's still there! . . . Callie, when did Biff and Chet leave?" He listened a moment. "Thanks. We can't locate them. . . . Nothing wrong for sure yet. We'll call you tomorrow."

Frank hung up and said worriedly, "They left the party ten minutes after we did."

Joe snapped his fingers. "I'll bet they couldn't get the jalopy started. They're probably spending the night with one of the fellows who lives on Callie's street."

Frank looked relieved. "Let's go over and check the jalopy." The boys began dressing.

"Have you a key to the car?" Mr. Hardy asked.

"Chet gave us one," Frank explained.

Fifteen minutes later the boys drove up quietly in their father's sedan and parked behind the yellow jalopy. Quickly Frank slipped into the driver's seat, and a moment later the Queen coughed and rattled into life. Abruptly he cut the motor and the two brothers looked at each other soberly.

"I was wrong," Joe said. "They didn't have car trouble. What *did* happen?"

Frank shook his head grimly. By the light of the street lamp the boys examined the jalopy, the curb and road around it, but found no clues. Using their flashlights, they checked the Shaws' yard and porch.

"Nothing here," Frank said finally.

The porch lights blinked on and Callie appeared in the doorway. "Frank—Joe, what are you doing?" she asked.

"Looking for clues," Joe replied. "But we haven't found any yet."

"Chet and Biff had their costumes on when they left, and carried the masks," Callie said. "They looked so conspicuous, they should be easy to locate."

"We'll keep trying," Frank promised.

He used the Shaw phone and called each boy who had been at the party. Chet and Biff were not with any of them, nor had Tony or Jerry heard from them.

Finally the Hardys headed for home. They gave their father the discouraging report and reluctantly went back to bed.

After a few hours of uneasy sleep, Frank and Joe awakened to find bright sunlight filling the room. Hurriedly they dressed and dashed downstairs. Their father was already at the breakfast table.

"Any news of Chet and Biff?" Frank asked.

Mr. Hardy shook his head soberly. "The police have found no trace of them."

"If only we knew where to start looking!" Joe said worriedly. "But we haven't a single clue to go on."

"The State Police are searching, too," Mr. Hardy told them. "A lead may turn up before the day is over. I hate to mention it," he added, "but the boys might have been kidnaped. So, to be on the safe side, there'll be absolutely no publicity."

"Good idea," Frank agreed.

For a minute he and Joe sat in glum silence. "What about the *Sleuth?*" Joe asked finally.

"The Coast Guard hasn't found it yet," Mr. Hardy replied, "and there are no leads on the bank robbery, either."

"How about the stolen car?" Frank queried. "Who owns it?"

"A man living up the coast," his father answered. "It disappeared day before yesterday while he was at a boat regatta in Northport."

"A boat regatta—" Joe murmured. "Where have we heard of one lately?"

"At the Coast Guard station," Frank prompted.

"That's it! Seaman Thompson thought the boat that tried to ram us might have come down from the regatta in Northport."

"Looks like Northport might furnish a lead to more than one mystery," Frank declared. "Let's take a run up there and see if we can pick up a clue."

"If I go up the coast, I want to go in the *Sleuth!*" Joe answered firmly. "We must find her!"

At this point, Mrs. Hardy brought the discussion to an end by setting before each boy a stack of steaming, golden-brown pancakes.

Aunt Gertrude came in behind her with a block of yellow butter and a tall pitcher of maple syrup. "There are more cakes on the griddle," she said.

"You need your strength. And for goodness' sake, find those poor lost boys!"

"If we can help—" Mrs. Hardy began.

"Thanks," Frank said.

After breakfast the brothers hurried to the garage. "The bank robbers must have beached the *Sleuth* somewhere," Joe reasoned. "If we follow the shore, we're sure to find her."

The black-and-silver motorcycles backfired like pistol shots, then roared from the drive and down High Street. The riders headed out Shore Road, past the private docks.

The fog of the night before had given way to a bright-blue summer morning. As the boys sped along in a cool, salty breeze they watched the white sand of the beach on their right. There was no sign of the *Sleuth*.

Finally they reached the head of the bay and turned sharply, following the seacoast northward. For a while Frank and Joe saw only the big green rollers of the Atlantic as they broke into foaming white along the sand and rocks.

The brothers spotted the squatters' colony of slapped-together board dwellings ahead.

The cycles chugged up Shore Road, which rose and twisted along the top of high, rocky cliffs along the sea.

"Look down there!" Joe called out suddenly. He had caught the glint of sunshine on a familiar hull. The *Sleuth!* It was stranded on the beach!

"Yippee!" exclaimed Frank. "The robbers must have floated her in at high tide." The boys parked their motorcycles and hurried to the edge of the bluff. Below them, the rocky cliff fell straight down to the boulders bordering the sand.

"I don't see a path," Frank said. "Wait! Here's a place we can go down."

As he leaned over the edge, a mass of loose sod and stone gave way at his feet. With a startled cry Frank slid downward. Desperately he grasped for a hold, his clawing fingers closing on a sharp slab jutting out just below the lip of the bluff. His body hung a hundred feet above the rocks and sand below.

"Hang on!" Joe shouted, and whipped his extra-long leather belt from its loops. Lying flat, he inched downward over the cliff edge until he could pass the leather under Frank's armpits. He slid the end through the buckle and pulled the belt tight.

Joe squirmed back again, braced himself, and hauled. For one sickening moment Frank swung like a pendulum beneath the cliff. With all his strength, Joe jerked the belt again and a moment later helped Frank clamber to safety.

"Whew! That was close!" Frank said, gasping. "If it hadn't been for you—"

"Better leave the boat," Joe panted, retrieving his belt. "We can come by sea with the Coast

Joe helped Frank clamber to safety

Guard and get her." Still shaking from fright, Frank agreed.

The brothers went at once to the Coast Guard station on the pier. When Lieutenant Parker heard Frank's story, he called two men and led the way to a patrol boat. The powerful craft headed straight out the mouth of the bay and turned sharply up the coast.

The beach was a whitish line on their left. Soon it broadened, and the tumble-down buildings of Shantytown came into view.

"Wait! Wait a minute!" Frank called out. "Can we slow down? What's that white thing floating in the water?"

"A dead fish," suggested a Coast Guardman.

The patrol boat throttled down and slid nearer the object. Leaning far over the side, Joe lunged and scooped it from the sea.

"This isn't a fish!" he cried out excitedly. "It's a rubber mask turned inside out!"

As he spoke, his fingers moved nimbly. In an instant a limp gorilla face appeared.

"This belongs to Chet!" Frank exclaimed.

CHAPTER VII

Dangerous Beachcombing

Frank took the mask from Joe and examined it carefully. "You're right. Here's the place where Chet ripped it at the party."

"But what's it doing floating in the bay?" asked Joe in great concern. "He and Biff must have gone out in a boat after all."

"But whose?" Frank queried.

"And why would they go out in the fog?" Joe added. Then he voiced the question uppermost in both their minds. "You don't think they could have drowned?"

Frank's face was grim. "Chet and Biff are excellent swimmers. Maybe, for a reason we don't know yet, they're hiding somewhere—perhaps Shantytown!" Frank gazed intently across the water at the squatter colony, now falling astern.

"Could be," Joe said. "They knew about our

case. Maybe they picked up a clue and landed in Shantytown. We'd better find out as soon as we get the *Sleuth*."

The boys lapsed into worried silence until the Coast Guard boat came within sight of rocky cliffs towering high above the white beach.

A seaman scanned the shore with binoculars and sang out, "There she is, sir! It's the *Sleuth*, all right. I can read her name."

The engines of the cutter shuddered as it swung in toward the beached motorboat. The Hardys whipped off their shoes and leaped overboard into thigh-deep water as the craft crunched against the sandy bottom. Joe was the first to reach the derelict *Sleuth*.

"She looks okay," he called out to his brother.

"Yes, but high and dry," Frank said as he waded ashore.

"We'll help you float her," a seaman offered.

Quickly gathering large pieces of driftwood, the boys improvised a crude skidway. Then, with the Coast Guardmen helping, they slid the boat down to the water. A towline was secured and the *Sleuth* bobbed toward Bayport in the wake of the Coast Guard patrol boat.

"Let's tow her straight to the boatyard," Frank suggested. "Maybe they have the new part by now."

His guess proved correct. While the patrol boat

waited, the young mechanic quickly examined the *Sleuth*.

"Have you been using her?" he asked the Hardys.

"Well—somebody has, Charlie," Joe replied.

The mechanic nodded. "Hm—thought so. The temporary repair I made didn't last. But if you keep turning the wheel, you can make her steer a little—enough to get by."

"That's how the bandits slipped away in the fog last night," Frank whispered to his brother.

"I'll be finished in an hour," Charlie said. "Shall I have her taken to your boathouse?"

"Righto," Frank replied. "We'll pick her up there."

The Hardys rode on the patrol boat to the Coast Guard pier, thanked Lieutenant Parker and his men for their help, and hastened to their motorcycles.

"I wish the *Sleuth* were ready now," Joe said impatiently, "so we could go right to Shanty-town."

"But first we have to round up beachcomber disguises," Frank reminded him.

The boys rode home and changed into dry clothes. While Mrs. Hardy and Aunt Gertrude were preparing lunch for them, Joe called police headquarters. He learned that there were no new leads on their friends or the bank robbers.

Chief Collig was amazed to hear about the discovery of Chet's mask. "The boys may be nearer than I thought. I've already sent out a seventeen-state missing-persons alarm."

"We might find more clues in Shantytown," Joe told him. "We're going there next."

Directly after lunch, Frank and Joe bounded upstairs, pulled out some old shirts and pants, and hurried down again. As they passed through the hall carrying the clothes, their mother and aunt looked out from the living room in surprise.

"Where are you going?" Aunt Gertrude inquired.

Mrs. Hardy asked, smiling, "Not another costume party? I returned your gorilla and magician suits this morning."

"Did you explain to Mr. French about Chet and Biff? He'll wonder why they don't bring their costumes back," Joe said.

"He wasn't there," Mrs. Hardy replied. "I left your outfits with the clerk."

"Where are you boys off to?" Aunt Gertrude demanded again.

"We're going sleuthing in Shantytown," Frank replied. "Probably we won't be home to supper."

Aunt Gertrude stared in disapproval. "Even foolhardy young detectives get hungry," she said tartly.

"I'll pack your supper," their mother offered. Aunt Gertrude and the boys followed her into the kitchen where the two women quickly prepared a package of food for the boys to take along.

"You and Auntie certainly move fast, Mother," Joe said admiringly. "Thanks a lot."

"Yes, we appreciate it," Frank chimed in.

Mrs. Hardy smiled. "We know you're in a hurry."

The boys went out the back door and hastily stowed the food and clothing in their motorcycle carriers.

"We must put in the make-up kit from the lab," Frank reminded his brother. With Fenton Hardy's help, Frank and Joe had fitted out a small modern crime laboratory over the family garage. Joe hurried upstairs to it and soon emerged with the kit, which he put in the carrier.

When they reached their boathouse, the boys found the *Sleuth* there. By the time the craft emerged, she carried two entirely different-looking young men.

Frank's face was smudged and his dark hair was tousled. He wore a battered straw hat and a striped jersey with a long rip in the back.

Joe's normal suntan had been made even darker by the use of make-up. A fake tattoo decorated his right arm. His trousers were torn off at the knees.

Both boys wore tennis shoes bursting at the sides. They carried burlap sacks appropriate for beachcombing.

"Let's land about a mile this side of Shanty-town," Frank suggested. "We can wander toward it along the beach."

Soon Beachcomber Joe, at the wheel, ran the *Sleuth* into a little cove. Drawing her up between two rocks, they camouflaged the craft with pieces of driftwood and dry seaweed.

"Now," said Joe, "if we can just find another clue to lead us to Chet and Biff!"

Frank nodded. "And at the same time learn what's behind the fighting in Shantytown."

Trying not to appear hurried, the two boys sauntered along with their sacks. The midafter-noon sun threw a white sparkle over everything —the curling waves, the sand, and even the gray, bleaching driftwood. Now and again Frank and Joe would stoop and put a handful of shells, bits of rope, or a few pebbles into the sacks.

"Some beachcombing!" Joe grinned.

At last the Hardys entered the squatters' village. The first huts were merely tarpaulins stretched across driftwood poles. But as the boys strolled along, they saw that several of the many shacks were of wood, well constructed, with solid, padlocked doors.

A few men were lounging about, smoking. Frank and Joe passed near a group roasting pota-toes in hot coals before one of the huts. The men paid no attention to the Hardys as the boys moved on.

"If Chet and Biff are here, they could be in any of these shacks!" Joe muttered in a low tone. "How can we get a closer look?"

The young sleuths were walking between the water's edge and the first row of huts. Near them a man stood in the water wringing out a shirt.

"Let's drift up to the next shack," Frank suggested.

The boys approached a solidly built shanty. Abruptly the door swung open. A thin, seedy-looking man with faded red hair stepped out in the sunlight and stared at them with hard blue eyes. As the Hardys returned the look, the fellow moved toward them.

"What are you doing here?" he challenged harshly.

"Just walking along the beach," Joe returned in a tough-sounding voice. "Looking for junk."

"Yeah? Well, get out of here and do it some place else. See?"

"This is a free country," Frank retorted, also speaking in a tough tone. "We'll walk here if we feel like it."

Instead of answering, the man reached into a back pocket and pulled out a blackjack. He lunged at Frank with the agility of a cat.

"Cut it out, Sutton!" barked a voice. The newcomer, a broad-shouldered young man, darted between Frank and his assailant. A boxer's hand chop sent the blackjack flying to the sand.

Sutton muttered under his breath, clenched his fists, and glared at the tall man. He was young and strong, with a blond crew cut.

"If you're looking for trouble, I'll give it to you," the big fellow said meaningfully.

Sutton dropped his eyes and turned away. He retrieved his weapon and disappeared behind his shanty.

Relieved, Frank said, "Thanks a lot, Mr.—"

"Call me Alf," was the friendly reply. "I was wading over there when I saw Sutton go for you. You'd better stay away from this place. We've had a lot of trouble lately."

"Well, thanks again, Alf," Frank said warmly as he shook the huge, hard hand. "You sure saved me a lump on the head. I'm Frank, and this is my brother Joe."

The three strolled along the beach. "So there's been trouble in Shantytown lately," Joe repeated, hoping to learn more from their new acquaintance.

"Yes. Sutton and his pals have been the ones making it, too. All they do is fight among themselves. Shantytown wouldn't be such a bad place, otherwise."

"Do you live here, Alf?" Frank inquired.

"Me?" The man laughed good-naturedly. "No, but I work on the docks and I know some fellows who work in town occasionally and live here, so I come out a lot on my hours off."

By now the three had reached the far edge of the colony. "I've got to see a fellow," Alf told them. "Look out for Hank Sutton when you go back. If he tries anything, just yell for Alf—Alf Lundborg."

The young giant's friendly act and his open face made Frank decide to trust him. "Maybe we can help you sometime, Alf," he said. "Our name is Hardy, but we don't want anyone in Shantytown to know it."

"Nobody'll hear it from me," Lundborg replied. "Say, if you're going to be around for a while, why don't you eat with my friends and me?"

"We'd like that," Frank said. "How'll we find you?"

Alf reached into his pocket. "Just listen for this," he replied, opening his hand. In the palm lay a harmonica. "See you around," he said and moved off.

When Alf Lundborg had gone up the beach, the brothers retraced their steps. While picking up more stones and shells, they scanned the sand carefully for anything that might belong to their missing chums. This time they took care not to venture too close to Sutton's shanty.

"There's our 'friend,'" Frank said in a low voice.

Stealing a glance toward the hut, Joe saw Sutton standing at one corner, talking earnestly with another man. His companion was listening with obvious impatience. He shifted his weight and suddenly turned full around. The Hardys saw that he was short in build, and had black hair combed straight back.

"That man!" Joe whispered. "It's—"

"I know!" Frank took his brother's arm and hurried him toward the beach. "It's the speedboat driver who almost rammed us! What's he doing here?"

CHAPTER VIII

Postcard Puzzle

"Keep going," Frank advised Joe. "If we turn around for another look, that powerboat pilot may recognize us!"

With bent heads, the young detectives shuffled along the beach between the ocean and the first line of squatters' shacks. If the stranger with the dark, combed-back hair noticed them at all, he saw only two ragged beachcombers wandering back in the direction of Bayport.

"So, the fellow who rammed us hangs around Shantytown!" Joe burst out.

"Yes," Frank added thoughtfully, "and he's friendly with the chief troublemaker there."

"But why should one of Sutton's pals try to ram the *Sleuth?*" Joe puzzled. "Because he found out—or suspected—we'd be investigating Shanty-town?"

"Possibly," Frank replied. "And if Chet and

Biff are prisoners here, the men don't want us to find out! They'll do everything to keep us away."

Joe whistled. "If that's true, we must find them. I'm scared about what may have happened to them."

"Maybe we'll pick up some clues tonight," Frank said. "It's almost suppertime. Let's go back and watch Sutton's place."

When the boys returned to the group of shacks, they saw some of the men drifting in from work, and others tending cooking fires.

Behind Sutton's shanty was a deserted shack. Frank and Joe slipped inside and settled themselves by a broken window. Although they stayed at their post an hour, they saw no sign of activity.

"Sutton's probably eating somewhere else," Frank said. "Let's find Alf and come back later."

As the boys stepped outside they heard a lively tune from a harmonica. Following the sound of the music, they found Alf playing for a small group of rough-looking men, seated around a fire.

When Alf finished the song, he introduced the boys and the laborers by first names. The men looked the Hardys over and nodded.

"The stew's done," a big red-faced man said, taking the lid from a large kettle. "Pitch in!"

As the men began to serve themselves on tin plates, Frank and Joe reached into their bags and took out the food they had brought. They unpacked a pound of frankfurters, rolls, two cans of beans, and apples.

"Help yourselves," Frank invited cordially.

"Looks good, boys," said the red-faced man, whose name was Lou. "Most of us are hungry enough to eat two suppers."

By the time the last crumb had disappeared, the men had warmed up to Frank and Joe and willingly answered their seemingly casual questions about Shantytown. None of the men, however, knew what the fights were about, nor had they seen two strange boys.

"We'll keep our eyes open for 'em," Lou volunteered. He took some driftwood from a bushel basket beside him, and threw two pieces on the fire. Then he tossed a piece of dark cloth after it.

"What's that?" Frank asked sharply. He grabbed a long stick and hooked the cloth from the blaze.

"It's just some junk I picked up," Lou answered.

Frank dropped it to the ground and the brothers eagerly examined the piece.

"It's a sleeve from Chet's gorilla outfit!" Joe whispered excitedly.

"I thought it looked familiar," Frank said. To Lou he said, "It's part of a costume. Where did you find this?"

"Behind Sutton's shack," the man replied.

"Is it important?" Alf asked the boys.

"It definitely links our missing friends with

Shantytown," Frank replied, as he put the sleeve in his burlap bag. "Come on, Joe! Let's go back to Sutton's place."

After thanking the men for their hospitality, the boys hurried off into the darkness.

"Be careful," Alf called after them. "Yell if you need help."

The Hardys found the shanty dark and padlocked. They circled it cautiously, but there was no one around. Joe knocked on the door. "Chet! Biff!" Frank called. Not a sound from inside. Again Joe pounded and both boys called repeatedly.

"It's no use," Joe said finally. "If they are inside, they're probably bound and gagged."

"Look for an opening between the boards," Frank instructed. The boys pulled out pencil flashlights and examined the side of the shack.

"I've found a knothole," said Joe.

"And here's a chink. I'll shine my light in while you look through the hole."

Joe watched the slender beam shift around the dark room. "Empty," he declared, disappointed. "Let's look for more of Chet's or Biff's belongings." They searched the sand around the shanty, but found nothing.

"Let's hide in the deserted shack again," Frank suggested. "If Sutton comes back with any of his pals, we may overhear something important."

Patiently the young detectives waited and watched, but their quarry did not return. Frank consulted his watch. "It's almost midnight. Maybe—"

"Sh!" Joe interrupted. "Listen!"

They heard footsteps and saw a dark figure approaching Sutton's shanty. The stranger knocked several times. Finally a neighbor opened his door. "You lookin' for Sutton?" he asked.

"Yes," replied the unknown caller.

"All I know is he went off in a car with a dark-haired fellow. I heard Sutton say he wouldn't come back tonight."

Without a word the caller disappeared into the darkness. The door to the shack slammed shut.

"That's that," Frank said in disappointment. "Let's go back to town and report to headquarters."

"You bet. Frank, do you suppose Chet and Biff were here but have been taken away?"

"It's a good guess."

The boys covered the mile of beach to their boat, quickly pulled off the improvised camouflage, and launched her. Frank headed down the coast toward Bayport and the Hardy boathouse. When the boys had debarked, they donned their street clothes again. Carrying their burlap bags, they emerged from the boathouse and mounted their motorcycles. It was well past midnight.

When the Hardys reached police headquarters, they were amazed to see Chief Collig in his office. He looked tired and somewhat dejected.

"I've been working night and day on the bank robbery case and the mystery of your friends," he said. "I'm afraid that the boys have been kidnaped."

"That's what we fear," Frank said. He showed the gorilla head mask and sleeve of Chet's costume and told of the boys' run-in with Sutton.

"I'll send men out there to make a thorough search," Collig said.

"We'll go with them!" Joe volunteered eagerly.

"We'd better not," Frank countered. "Once the men at Shantytown see us with the police, we won't be able to work under cover there."

Regretfully, Joe agreed.

Chief Collig rose, strode around the desk, and clapped each of the young sleuths on the shoulder. "Thanks, boys! You've brought in the first two leads I've had on this case," he said. "If we find Chet and Biff, I'll call you at once."

Frank and Joe hurried home through the silent streets. When they let themselves into the house, they saw a light in Fenton Hardy's upstairs study. Frank knocked.

"Come in," called the detective. When his sons entered, he pushed aside some papers on his desk. "What did you find out today?"

He leaned back in his big leather chair and listened carefully as his sons gave an account of their day's progress.

When it was finished, their father said, "If Collig doesn't find Chet and Biff in Shantytown tonight, and they were kidnaped, their parents should receive ransom notes soon."

"Perhaps they will come tomorrow," Frank suggested. He turned to his father. "Do you think Chet and Biff's disappearance could have anything to do with the bank robbery?"

"It's possible."

"In that case, maybe you'd let us give you a hand on the bank robbery case, Dad."

"As a matter of fact," the detective replied, "if Collig hadn't offered you the Shantytown problem, I would have asked your help on this one."

Frank and Joe looked perplexed. "But the bank robbery hadn't happened then!" Joe protested.

Mr. Hardy smiled briefly. "For some time I have been working secretly to round up a certain ring of bank robbers who operate on a national scale."

"I see," said Frank. "And they committed the Bayport holdup?"

"I believe so. It looks like their work. I've learned that the gang is broken up into a number of teams," Mr. Hardy explained. "Somewhere on the West Coast is the ringleader who assigns each 'team' to rob a local bank in a different part of the country. The scheme is very well organized."

The boys went to bed, hoping to be disturbed by a call from the police, telling them good news, but none came. In the morning Joe called headquarters, then relayed a disappointing report to his family. "The police didn't find Chet and Biff, but they picked up pieces of their costumes on piles of half-charred paper trash in different parts of Shantytown. Someone didn't know the outfits were fireproof and tried to burn them."

"Then our pals *were* taken there and later moved somewhere else," Frank declared. "But where?"

He and Joe were so upset they could hardly eat breakfast. The other Hardys, who also were fond of Chet and Biff, were greatly sobered.

"Oh, I almost forgot something," said Mrs. Hardy. "A letter came for you boys in this morning's early mail." She handed Frank a plain white envelope. "It's postmarked Northport, yesterday."

Frank looked at it. "The writing is familiar," he remarked, "but there's no return address."

He tore open the envelope, took out a picture postcard, and scanned the message.

Frank's eyes widened. "Listen to this!" he exclaimed. " 'Having a wonderful time. Don't worry about us.' And it's signed 'Chet and Biff'!"

The rest of the family stared in amazement.

Aunt Gertrude snorted indignantly. "Having a wonderful time, indeed! Everyone worried sick, police searching all over the map for them, and they're having a wonderful time!"

"But what a relief!" Mrs. Hardy said warmly. "I'll call Mrs. Morton and—"

"Wait a minute," Mr. Hardy cautioned. "It may not really be from the boys."

"This is Chet's handwriting," Frank said.

Joe had jumped from his chair to examine the card. "Yes, it is," he affirmed. "The picture is of Waterfront Street in Northport. Looks like an old card," he added, passing it to his father.

"Why do you think it was mailed in an envelope?" Mrs. Hardy asked, puzzled.

"So no one would read the message until it got here," suggested Joe.

"Why didn't they telephone?" Aunt Gertrude asked tartly. "It's even quicker."

"I think they would if they could, Auntie," Frank replied. "Chet and Biff know better than to worry everybody this way. They're prisoners!"

"Anyway, we know they're alive," said his mother. "That in itself is good news."

"Will you call Mrs. Hooper and Mrs. Morton and tell them?" Frank requested his mother. She nodded.

"And I'll notify the police," Mr. Hardy added. "By the way, they looked for the thieves' fingerprints on Chet's jalopy and your motorboat, but didn't find any."

"I suppose the robbers wore gloves," Frank remarked.

As Joe went back to his chair, he said, "I think we ought to run up to Northport and see if we can trace this card."

Mr. Hardy looked thoughtful. "The bank robbers stole their getaway car in Northport."

"And the fellow who tried to ram the *Sleuth*," Frank added, "may have come down from there after watching the regatta."

"Don't forget," said Joe, "he's a pal of Sutton's."

"Northport might provide clues to Chet and Biff, the bank robbery, and the Shantytown trouble," Frank concluded.

The boys finished their breakfast and rode to the Hardy boathouse. As Joe stepped into the *Sleuth,* he kicked off his moccasins. The next moment he cried, "Ouch—hey! Broken glass!" He lifted the floor rack. "There's a whole mess of it in the bottom. Looks like a soda bottle."

"That's funny," said Frank. "We didn't notice any yesterday."

"That's because the glass was all hidden under the rack," Joe pointed out. "This piece was forced up between the slats overnight by the rocking of the boat."

While he gingerly extracted a sliver of glass

from his toe, Frank picked up the jagged fragments. "These weren't here the day before the robbery," he broke in excitedly. "We took out the
rack and emptied the boat completely. It's a clue,
Joe! We'll put these pieces together at home."

He found some cheesecloth in the dashboard
compartment, gathered all the glass fragments
into it, and put the little bundle in his pocket.
Joe, meanwhile, stuck a small bandage on his foot
and put on his shoes.

After filling the tank with fuel, the boys headed
for Northport. The motorboat streaked across
the bay, with Frank at the wheel. Skillfully he
throttled down a bit as his craft moved into the
long, dark swells of the Atlantic.

Steadily the *Sleuth* plowed northward. Joe
shaded his eyes with his hand as dots of land appeared off the coast ahead. "There are the islands
where Chet and Biff wanted to camp," he noted.
"Say! They're pretty isolated—and would be
likely spots for hiding kidnap victims! We ought
to search them if we don't find some clue to the
boys in Northport."

"I'll pass them as close as I can," Frank offered.
"Maybe we'll see something."

One by one the line of islets could be seen.
Though the Hardys watched carefully, they saw
only sand, pines, and huge stone formations.
Some of the islands were surrounded by dangerous half-submerged rocks.

"We're getting close to Jagged Reef," Joe reminded his brother. "Better take her out. Those rocky teeth can bite the bottom of a boat!"

Frank turned the *Sleuth's* prow seaward. As he revved up the engine, however, he was startled by a shout from Joe.

"Hold it! There—submerged just off those rocks—" Joe pointed to a little island. "It looks like the wreck of a motorboat!"

Immediately Frank throttled down and headed toward the spot. Finally he let the engine idle. "I don't dare go any closer," he said. "Can you see her from here?"

"Only the outline," reported Joe, who was standing up now with one foot on the gunwale. "Looks as if she hit a rock close to shore and sank. She's a good size."

"Those fragments on the rock look black," Joe noticed. "So does the outline. Say, do you suppose it's the boat that nearly hit us—the *Black Cat?*"

"We can find out," Frank said promptly. "Our underwater equipment is in the locker. Take the wheel. I want to get a look."

Quickly Frank donned a face mask with a wide glass plate. Leaning over, he put his head in the water and strained to see the wreck more clearly.

Lifting his face, he exclaimed, "It *is* black! I can't tell if it's the *Black Cat* at this distance. Keep her in close, Joe. Why are we drifting away?"

"Can't help it." Desperately Joe yanked at the wheel. "We're caught in the current!" he exclaimed frantically.

While the boys had been intent on the sunken hull, the swift, strong current had caught their craft. The *Sleuth* was being rushed toward the deadly rocks of Jagged Reef!

CHAPTER IX

The Old Salt's Story

BUFFETED by the current, the *Sleuth* plunged out of control toward the line of white exploding spray, where the sea's swell smacked against the barrier reef.

Joe bore down hard on the wheel as the churned-up waters, falling back from the rocks, seethed underneath. The din of crashing waves was terrific, but above it could be heard the powerful throb of the *Sleuth*'s engine.

"If I could only turn her!" Joe thought.

For an instant the motorboat seemed to stand still in the midst of the boiling waters. The engine and treacherous current pulled with equal strength in a fierce tug of war. Then, slowly, the sturdy craft inched her way seaward under Joe's guidance.

"She did it!" Frank whooped in relief. "What a boat! And nice piloting, Joe!"

The *Sleuth* gathered speed and Joe took the boat out a safe distance from the reef.

"Too bad we couldn't find out if that sunken boat was the *Black Cat*," he remarked. "But maybe we can learn something about the wreck when we get to Northport."

"First we should trace the postcard," Frank said. He pulled it from his pocket and looked at it again carefully. "This is so old, it probably was bought in a place that doesn't sell many," he commented.

"The edges are yellow and the picture is out of date. There haven't been trolleys on Waterfront Street for years. As soon as we get there, let's look for a little hole-in-the-wall store."

Frank studied the card from all angles. "Joe, look!" he exclaimed, and pointed to the thin edge. There was a blue stain. "Ink," Frank judged. "If it was spilled on the whole batch of cards, the others will have similar blots. We'll look for that."

It was well past noon when the boys sighted Northport on their left. Passing between a pair of entrance buoys, the *Sleuth* came off the swelling ocean onto the calm surface of a small, well-protected harbor.

On one side a forest of thick masts rose from a fleet of sturdy fishing boats. At the far end of the bay, bright-colored pleasure craft rode at anchor. Slender, pencillike masts marked the sailboats. On the shore nearby were the yellow wooden skeletons of boats under construction.

Joe guided the *Sleuth* toward a large dock with gasoline pumps, which extended into the water from the boatyard.

"This must be the yard that sponsored the regatta," Frank commented. "Bring her in, Joe."

Within minutes the young detectives had made their craft secure and scrambled onto the dock. They hurried down the wooden planking and turned onto Waterfront Street. There were restaurants, souvenir shops, and boat-supply stores. All of them were well kept and busy. The boys stopped in a luncheonette for a snack, then hurried on. They paused to look down the first intersecting street. It was narrow and shabby.

"Let's try the stores on this street," Joe suggested.

Halfway down the block, they found a small confectionery squeezed between a junk shop and an empty store. There was a sign HARRY's on the window.

As the boys went in, a musty smell hit them. When their eyes adjusted from bright sunlight to the dark interior, they saw a glass case of candy and a soda fountain with a broken stool. There was no one in the store.

"Look!" Frank said, pointing to a rack of postcards on a shelf behind the candy case.

As Joe stepped behind the counter to peer at

them, a door opened in the rear of the store.

"Don't touch!" said a deep voice.

The boys turned to see a big man lumbering toward them. He had a swarthy face with huge dark eyes and a heavy black mustache.

"You want a postcard?" he asked shortly.

"Yes, please," Joe replied. The shopkeeper took the card rack from the shelf and placed it on the counter. "Pick out," he ordered.

Frank showed the man Chet's postcard. "We want one like this. Some friends of ours bought it here yesterday, we think."

The man looked at them stonily. "Could be!" He pointed at the rack to some faded cards identical to the one Frank held. Joe lifted them out, held them up together, and squinted at the edges. There was the blue inkstain!

"Do you remember the fellows who bought this one?" Frank asked casually, holding out the card from Chet and Biff.

"You buying or asking questions?" the man inquired.

"Both," Frank told him with a smile.

"I guess you don't recall," Joe said. "Two boys our age—one of them pretty chubby?"

The man looked annoyed. "I remember who comes in my place," he said hotly. "No kids. It was a big, bald fellow with a loud voice. He bought a lot of Fizzle soda. Second time in a week."

Frank and Joe exchanged glances. Both had the

same recollection: the huge, bald-headed man in the *Black Cat*. Could he be the postcard purchaser?

Unable to learn more, the boys thanked the proprietor and purchased three postcards. Outside, they turned toward Waterfront Street.

"Just as we suspected!" Joe burst out. "The postcard's a phony. Somebody forced Chet and Biff to write it!"

"And that somebody may be the bald man. But what's his game? And is his buddy who piloted the *Black Cat* in on it too? What's their connection with Shantytown, anyway?"

"I'd sure like to get my hands on those two guys!" Joe declared. "They must know where Biff and Chet are."

The Hardys stopped at a nearby restaurant, where Frank telephoned Bayport police headquarters. He gave a report of their findings to Chief Collig.

"Good lead," said the officer. "That bald fellow might have a connection with your pals' disappearance. I'll send out a description of him. Keep up the good work."

The Hardys then went to the boatyard where they had left the *Sleuth*. "Maybe someone here knows about the *Black Cat*," Joe said. "Let's ask."

As the boys walked out on the docks, a wiry man bustled up to greet them. He had a lively, ruddy face and unruly black hair.

"Hello, mates!" he called out. "I'm William Caine—I manage this dock. Need any gas? Repairs?"

Frank spoke up. "What we really want, Mr. Caine, is some information."

The manager smiled. "We've got plenty of that, too. Come along."

The friendly man led the Hardys to his office, an old deck cabin, at one end of his dock. Inside, Frank and Joe looked about them curiously. The room was filled with all sorts of old sea articles—a barometer, a binnacle, and a huge pilot wheel. In addition, there were a desk, a filing cabinet, a typewriter, and a telephone.

"Pretty snug, eh?" Mr. Caine chuckled. "It's my little bit of sea on shore, now that my sailing days are over."

While Joe grinned appreciatively, Frank noted a limp object lying on top of the filing cabinet. "Excuse me, Mr. Caine," he said. "What's that?"

The seafaring man followed Frank's gaze. "Oh, that!" Carelessly he tossed it over.

"A mask!" Frank exclaimed.

"A gorilla mask!" Joe added. "Where did you get this, Mr. Caine?"

"Kind of scary, ain't he?" The old-timer chuckled. "We had a big masquerade party the last night of the regatta. I went as a gorilla."

The young sleuths studied the rubber face intently. "Coincidence," Joe murmured.

"Sure was a big regatta," the manager went on. "People came from all over."

Joe nodded. "What we want to ask you about, Mr. Caine, is a good-sized inboard, painted all black, named the *Black Cat*."

"The *Black Cat*?" Caine raised his eyebrows. "Why, I own her!"

"You do?" Frank exclaimed.

"Sure. Nice fast boat, too. Where'd you see her?"

"At Bayport, day before yesterday," Joe replied. "She tried to ram us."

Caine looked astonished. "What happened?"

"We pulled away from her."

"You fellows must have a pretty good boat yourselves!"

"Who was piloting the *Black Cat*, Mr. Caine?" Frank asked. "Did he wreck her?"

"I should say not! She's tied up to the dock right this minute."

"We saw the sunken hull of a black boat off one of the islands," Joe explained.

"Oh, yes, the poor old *Queen of Spades*," Mr. Caine replied. "Too bad she was wrecked. Like to have a look at my boat?"

"We sure would!" Joe declared.

Caine obligingly led the way out on the long pier. As he walked, the old salt rambled on about the *Black Cat*. "She's a fast boat, all right. Let's see—day before yesterday—that was the last day of the regatta. Three men from San Francisco hired her."

"Three?" Joe caught him up. "There were only two men aboard when they tried to ram our boat."

"Well, three hired her, but only two went out in her. Let's see—there were the Stark brothers, Ben and Fritz, I think their names were, and a third fellow—big and bald. He and Ben went out in the boat. The men said they came all the way here on their vacations, especially to see the regatta."

"Are they still around?" Frank asked.

"They're back in California by now, I guess," Caine replied. "Said they were taking a plane." He stopped at the edge of the dock and motioned downward. "There she is," he said proudly.

Frank and Joe found themselves looking into the same sleek, black powerboat which had nearly rammed them.

Joe stepped into the boat and looked around carefully. "Sure they didn't leave anything behind?"

"Yep. I always clean my boats out good after people bring 'em in."

"Well, the *Black Cat* sure is a nice boat," Joe declared as he climbed back onto the dock. "Which one of the renters was driving her? A dark fellow, with black hair combed straight back?"

"Yes," Caine replied. "That would be Ben Stark."

"We reported the attack to the Coast Guard," Frank told the manager.

"And right you were!" said Mr. Caine. "Just let them turn up here again, and I'll have 'em arrested."

"If you should hear anything about them, please let us know," Frank requested, and gave his name and address.

"Glad to!" exclaimed Caine. "Now can I give you some gas?"

"We'd better get some," Frank replied, "and start for home."

By the time the boys were ready to leave, the sun was setting. Frank revved up the *Sleuth*'s power plant and sent the craft knifing through the swells.

Soon the boys passed out the narrow mouth of Northport harbor. Frank turned the *Sleuth* southward toward Bayport.

The sea was calmer than it had been during the day. On the ocean's horizon the darkness gathered slowly, and finally a few stars were beginning to push through when the coastal islands came into view on the *Sleuth*'s starboard side.

After passing Jagged Reef safely, Frank ran in closer to the islands. Ahead they saw a tall, limp white sail. As the *Sleuth* drew nearer, the boys made out the masts and hull of a trim-looking schooner, anchored for the night off one of the islets.

"Nice lines," commented Joe. "Pass close to her, will you, Frank?"

Quietly, with her engine throttled down, the motorboat drew abreast of the larger vessel. It was now dusk and a light shone in her cabin from which came the sound of activity. Frank gazed in admiration at the tall masts and shipshape rigging.

Suddenly Joe's fingers clutched his brother's shoulder. "Look! On the deck!"

As the *Sleuth* passed the schooner, Frank caught a quick glimpse of the figure of a boy leaning over the rail.

Joe cried out, "That was Chet!"

CHAPTER X

A Narrow Escape

"It's either Chet or his double!" Joe exclaimed. "But I'm sure my eyes weren't playing tricks."

"Do you suppose he's a prisoner on that schooner?" Frank asked. "Well, we'll soon find out!"

He turned the wheel sharply and the *Sleuth* swung about. It circled close to the anchored vessel.

"Chet!" cried Joe, making a trumpet of his hands. "Chet Morton! It's Frank and Joe! Are you all right?"

"*Che-e-t!*" both boys yelled together. "*Che-e-t Mo-or-ton!*"

A momentary hush followed, as the Hardys paused for breath. All sounds of activity aboard the schooner ceased. Abruptly a burly sailor in white duck trousers appeared on deck.

"What's all the holler?" he barked. "Clear out of here, or you'll get in plenty of trouble!"

As Joe stood up to retort, Frank yanked him down again. "We should go!" he whispered. "Let him think he scared us off."

The *Sleuth*'s engine roared louder, and the boat moved along the shore of the island until the white sails were out of sight.

"It'll be black night out here in half an hour," Frank explained. "Then we'll go back and see what's up."

Daylight faded away, leaving in its place broadly sprinkled stars. A calm ocean swayed their boat gently. Rocks along the shore humped up, massive shapes in the darkness.

"Now!" Frank said softly.

Joe took the wheel and throttled the smooth-running engine so low that its sound was only a faint hum. Keeping as close to shore as possible, the *Sleuth* crept toward the anchored schooner.

When the vessel loomed just ahead, Joe cut the throttle completely and the motorboat glided noiselessly under her stern. Frank, holding out his hands to ward off the hull, suddenly felt rough fibers.

"A rope ladder!" he whispered. "I'm going up!"

"I'll follow," said Joe.

After securing their own boat with a loose hitch, Frank cautiously drew his body upward, rung by rung. Joe was right behind him. Frank slipped underneath the rail and crawled along the empty deck.

Joe reached the top of the ladder and stepped forward. Suddenly, from out of the darkness, two powerful arms seized him in a viselike grip, and a man's sandpaper voice called out:

"Here! I caught one of them!"

Joe tensed in surprise, then spun around, breaking the grip. He ducked. With all his strength he drove upward, his head hitting the midsection of his attacker like a battering ram.

As the man fell back, gasping, Joe leaped to his feet. "Frank!" he cried hoarsely. There was no reply, but a wild clamor rose from the fore part of the deck.

"Here he is!" someone cried out.

"No, here!" another rasped.

"That's me, you fool!"

Someone began ringing the deck bell. There came the shuffle of running feet and the grunting of men short of breath.

Then Frank's clear voice sang out, "No use, Joe! Overboard!"

Both boys vaulted the rail. As Joe hit the water, another geyser of spray rose several feet from him. The Hardys popped to the surface, then disappeared under the dark water again.

"Harbor thieves!" came shouts from the deck. "Get them!" The bell clanged on. There were

"Harbor thieves! Get them!" came shouts
from the deck

two sudden bursts of light, accompanied by sharp explosions. Someone was shooting wildly!

Frank and Joe surfaced near the rope ladder and quickly untied the *Sleuth*. Swimming with swift, silent strokes they pushed their craft away from the schooner into the protecting darkness.

"Whew!" breathed Joe as he tumbled, panting, into the motorboat. "They must have been on deck, watching."

"Anyhow, I found out what we wanted to know," Frank reported. "That wasn't Chet, but a boy who looks a lot like him."

"How do you know?"

"He tackled me. I said, 'Chet, it's Frank!' but he hung on tightly. That's when I yelled for you to go over the side."

Joe started the motor and opened the throttle all the way. As the *Sleuth* gained power, the prow lifted and the boat leaped forward. Safely away from the yacht, Joe switched on the running lights. Along the shore, they could see a solitary light here and there. Presently the bright glow of beach fires told them they were passing Shantytown.

"No more stops tonight," Frank said with a chuckle.

The *Sleuth* crossed the quiet expanse of Bayport harbor and finally entered their boathouse. Twenty minutes later they reached the Hardy house. Their mother and aunt were anxiously waiting.

"Goodness gracious!" scolded Aunt Gertrude. "Is this a time to come home—" She stopped and gasped. "Oh! Look at them! Soaking wet—like a pair of drowned rats!"

"We're almost dry, Auntie," Joe replied with a laugh. "We fell in over an hour ago."

"Fell in!" their mother exclaimed. "We can't wait to hear! But first you'd better go upstairs and change, then have some supper."

Soon Frank and Joe, comfortable in fresh, dry clothes, were seated at the kitchen table before a late but steaming dinner.

"Where's Dad?" Frank asked.

"He left town this afternoon," Mrs. Hardy replied. "He's checking an out-of-state clue on the bank robbery. Now tell us what happened to you boys."

"Well, we thought we saw Chet on a schooner," Frank began, as he cut into a generous slice of roast beef.

"Only it wasn't Chet . . ." Joe said, and helped himself to a baked potato.

"They thought we were thieves . . ." Frank tried again.

"So we jumped overboard!" Joe added.

"A very clear account," Aunt Gertrude commented tartly.

As soon as the brothers finished eating they excused themselves, jumped up, and headed for the back door.

"Oh, no!" cried Aunt Gertrude in alarm. "Where are you off to now?"

"Just out to the laboratory, Auntie," Frank reassured her. "We found something today we must work on."

The boys ran up the garage stairs and Joe unlocked the door at the top. Frank switched on the fluorescent light over a clean table. On it he laid the cheesecloth bundle of glass fragments from the *Sleuth.*

"We'll need something to hold these together," he noted, unwrapping the green shards. As the brothers examined them, Frank reached for a container of putty. "This will be better than glue."

Treating the fragments like pieces in a jigsaw puzzle, the young sleuths rebuilt a twelve-ounce, green-tinted pop bottle.

"Fizzle," Joe read from the raised glass letters. "Fizzle—where—"

"Harry's confectionery in Northport!" Frank broke in excitedly. "The owner said that the bald man bought several bottles of Fizzle!"

"You mean *he* might have been the one who left the broken glass in the *Sleuth?*"

"Yes! Not only that—he might have done it while helping to steal our boat."

"Wait a minute!" Joe's thoughts raced as he

followed his brother's line of deduction. "If that's true, he could be one of the bank robbers! They stole a car in Northport!"

"And don't forget the postcard business, which may tie him in with the kidnaping of Chet and Biff!"

Joe nodded. "Then there's Ben Stark, the pilot of the *Black Cat,* which by the way, came down from Northport the day of the bank robbery. Is he linked with both cases? And is his pal Sutton? And where do the fights at Shantytown fit in?"

"That's for us to find out," Frank said determinedly. "Especially since the answer might lead us to Chet and Biff. We're pretty sure they *were* in Shantytown—since we found Chet's gorilla mask off the coast there, and his sleeve was picked up behind Sutton's shack."

The excitement suddenly faded from Joe's face. "Maybe our hunches are on the wrong track. After all, Fizzle could be sold in other places besides Northport—and we have no proof the bald guy left the bottle in the *Sleuth.*"

"Don't be a pessimist," Frank begged. "Remember what Dad says: 'Persistence is just as important as cleverness in detective work.' "

"Yes, and a little luck helps, too. Don't worry. It's just that we have so many mysteries to solve. Which one do we tackle next?" The ringing of the telephone interrupted. Frank answered.

"Glad to find you home," came Chief Collig's

familiar voice. "Maybe you can help me. We have a man down here—been brought in for stealing. He seems to think you and Joe can clear him."

"Joe and I?" repeated Frank, astonished. "Why . . . what's his name? What does he look like?"

"He's a big, strong fellow—a stevedore. Calls himself Alf."

CHAPTER XI

Midnight Caller

"ALF Lundborg a thief!" Frank exclaimed. "I can't believe it! We'll be right down, Chief Collig," he promised.

"I don't buy it," Joe said flatly as they started out. "What's the pitch?"

Frank shrugged and hurried off to inform his mother of the errand, while Joe locked the laboratory. Then the brothers rushed downtown on their motorcycles to Chief Collig's office.

"Where's Alf?" asked Joe, looking around as he entered.

"We're holding him in a cell until I talk to you boys," the officer explained.

"He's the man we told you about yesterday," Frank reminded the chief. "The one who helped us in Shantytown. If it hadn't been for him, Sutton would have cracked my skull with a blackjack."

"I remember," the chief replied. "Sutton's the

cause of his arrest." Before the surprised boys could speak, he added, "I'll let Lundborg tell you himself." Over his intercom he ordered the suspect brought in.

"I don't believe Alf's a thief," Frank said.

"But he does have a record for petty theft and disturbing the peace," Chief Collig said soberly. "That makes it look bad for him."

"How long ago was that?" Joe asked.

"Alf's last brush with the law was five years ago," Collig replied. "He claims he was just a wild kid at the time."

The door opened and Alf stood on the threshold. His giant frame almost hid the sergeant behind him. When he saw the Hardys, his troubled face lighted up instantly.

"I knew you fellows wouldn't let me down," he burst out. "Tell the chief I didn't take it!"

"Take what, Alf?" said Frank.

"The police found a transistor radio in my knapsack," the big man explained, "but I didn't put it there!"

"Sutton reported it stolen," the officer said. "We sent out Lieutenant Daley to investigate, and he found it in Lundborg's bag."

"Is Lieutenant Daley still here?" Frank asked. "Would you have him come in?" Collig nodded.

A few minutes later a tall, thin-faced officer entered. He and the Hardys had known one another for years and exchanged greetings. "Lieutenant

Daley," Frank said, "when you were hunting for the radio who suggested that you look in Alf's knapsack?"

"Sutton," the officer answered.

Frank nodded. "It looks like a plant, Chief."

"Sure it is," Joe declared. "Alf scared Sutton off when he attacked Frank. He probably planted the radio to get even."

"That's right! That's just what I told them!" Alf boomed. "Thanks a lot for sticking by me, fellows. I'll get Sutton!"

"Hold on there!" commanded Chief Collig. "You'll be back here for assault if you try that. Since the Hardys back up your story, I'll let you go. But if Sutton prosecutes, we'll have to bring you in again."

"Okay." Alf wrung the boys' hands, thanked them, and left.

Frank pointed to a radio on Collig's desk and asked, "Is this the stolen property?"

"That's it," Lieutenant Daley spoke up.

"Take a look," the chief invited, and Frank picked up the compact, heavy little set.

"Japanese make. Yokohama Super-X."

"Let's see," Joe requested. He gave a low whistle as his brother passed it to him. "What a little beauty! Brand new, too. Look at that nickel-and-ivory case!"

"It's an expensive, rare set," Lieutenant Daley commented. "Not many people can afford one."

"That's true," Frank said. "Hank Sutton seems to be just a seedy-looking character who lives in Shantytown. But Joe and I have a hunch as to how *he* could afford a radio like this."

"You mean he stole it?" Chief Collig asked.

"We think he belongs to a ring of thieves," Frank told him. "If they fight among themselves, it would explain the trouble in Shantytown."

Lieutenant Daley looked doubtful. "If Sutton stole the radio, why would he plant it on Alf? That would only call the attention of the police to himself."

Frank grinned. "If you'd seen Sutton go after me, you'd know he acts first and thinks later."

"Then he's probably regretting Lundborg's arrest right now," Lieutenant Daley returned.

"That's not all he'll regret," Joe promised grimly, "if he's had anything to do with Chet and Biff's disappearance."

"That reminds me," the chief said. "The boys' parents received postcards from Northport, too. We're looking for the bald, loud-voiced man you told me about, but that isn't much to go on."

"No," Frank admitted, "but we're working on a new clue." He told of the discovery of the Fizzle soda bottle and the purchase of a similar one by the bald-headed man in Northport. "That's why we think he's connected with stealing the *Sleuth* as well as Chet and Biff's disappearance."

"Then," Joe put in, "we learned that the dock

manager up there owns the *Black Cat* and rented it the day of the bank robbery to the bald fellow and Ben Stark—the one we saw talking to Hank Sutton in Shantytown."

Chief Collig looked at the boys keenly. "I see what you're driving at—that Sutton may be more than a petty thief—he and the other two might be involved in the robbery!"

As Lieutenant Daley stared at the Hardys in amazement, Frank replied, "You're right, Chief. But we have no solid evidence yet to back up our hunch. Joe and I will check stores in town tomorrow to see where the radio came from."

"Good. We'll do some checking of our own too. Thanks, Frank and Joe, for coming down."

When the Hardys reached home, their house was dark. They let themselves in quietly, went to bed, and fell asleep at once.

Some time later Joe was awakened by a noise. He sat up, listening. It came again—a soft knocking.

"Frank!" he whispered, shaking his brother. "Someone's at the front door."

Instantly Frank was awake. The boys hurried downstairs. As the gentle knocking began again, Frank switched on the porch light. Joe swung open the front door. Before them stood a tall, thin, worried-looking man.

"Mr. French!" cried Joe in surprise.

The costume dealer's mouth dropped open in

astonishment. "You—you're not—you're here!" he stammered incoherently.

"Yes, of course, we are," Frank responded. "Why are you so surprised to see us?"

"Why—ah—I'm terribly sorry, boys!" Mr. French looked nervously over his shoulder. "I—I see I've come to the wrong street—looking for High *Avenue,* and this must be High *Street.* So sorry! Good night!"

The tall man hurried down the steps to a car at the curb and drove away.

Joe turned to his brother. "There isn't any High Avenue in Bayport. Mr. French must know that. He's been in business here for years."

As Frank closed the door, they heard footsteps at the top of the stairs and their mother's voice asked softly, "What is it, Gertrude?"

"Burglars!" hissed their aunt. "I heard them talking." She called down in a loud but shaky voice, "The police are coming! Go or I'll call my nephews! Frank! Joe!"

"We're down here, Auntie!" Frank informed her, stifling a laugh. "There are no burglars."

After a second's pause there came a weak "Well!" followed by "Humph! I might have known!"

"What's the matter, boys?" Mrs. Hardy asked.

"Someone here who said he had the wrong street," Joe told her, and switched off the porch light.

The next morning the boys ate an early breakfast. Afterward, Frank suggested, "Let's try all the appliance stores to see if Sutton did buy the Super-X radio. We can see Mr. French later."

Joe agreed and they set off. They went from shop to shop, but the story was always the same: The merchants did not stock the Yokohama Super-X radio—it was too costly to sell many sets. At last, however, a young clerk in a hi-fi equipment store said, "Yes, we have them. I'll be glad to show you one."

"We're not here to buy," Frank said. "We just want to know if you've sold any recently."

"No," the disappointed clerk admitted. "We don't sell many. We thought we would—despite the high price—because the Super-X transistor has so many extra features—FM, short wave— name it!"

"Where do you get them?" Joe asked.

"We import directly from the Yokohama Radio Company's distributors in Japan. The radios come in by ship and are unloaded on the Bayport docks."

"Have you missed any from your stock lately?" Frank queried.

The clerk looked surprised, but answered readily, "No, but we were short one crate on the last shipment. My boss wrote to the distributor in Japan about it, but there hasn't been time for a reply yet."

The boys thanked the youth and returned to the street. They wondered about the clerk's remarks concerning the foreign-made radios.

"If Sutton bought the radio, he didn't buy it in Bayport," Joe declared.

Frank said, "He may have stolen the whole crate that was supposed to go to the hi-fi store. Let's cycle out to Shantytown. Maybe we can learn more about Sutton."

The brothers hurried home and put on their beachcomber clothes. Then they hopped onto their motorcycles and sped along Shore Road. They hid their cycles in a grove of short, scrubby pines near the squatter colony.

"We'd better walk the rest of the way," Joe said, "and act as casual as possible."

Frank and Joe entered the camp cautiously. It was noontime and pale smoke rose from a few cooking fires near the water. The village was nearly deserted and the boys judged that Sutton's shack was empty. The door was padlocked.

As Frank and Joe wandered among the huts, they noticed that each one had a trash heap of its own in the rear. Suddenly Joe darted to a pile in which something glinted in the sunlight.

"What did you find?" Frank called, and ran forward to look.

"Pop bottles!" Joe exulted, holding one aloft. "Fizzle soda!"

CHAPTER XII

The Desolate Island

JOE picked up another bottle from the rubbish heap. "It's exactly like the one we pieced together last night," he declared. "These *prove* the bank robbers are linked up with Shantytown!"

"It looks that way," Frank conceded. "But— Fizzle soda may be sold around Bayport. As you said, we don't know for certain that the robbers used the *Sleuth*. Somebody may just have 'borrowed' it for a joy ride."

"Well, the bottles make it *likely* that the robbers are connected to this place," Joe amended. "But let's scout around some more."

The two boys, hands in pockets, strolled casually among the shacks. Although they looked closely at the few squatters hanging around, they saw no one they recognized. Disappointed, the brothers circled back to the trash heap.

"We're getting nowhere," said Joe, disheartened.

Suddenly Frank's body tensed. "Sh! Listen! Hear that?"

"All I hear is the ocean."

"Someone is groaning!"

Still listening intently, Frank turned and looked all around him. The nearest building was a gray, windowless shack with a closed door. Abruptly he strode toward it, Joe behind him.

Reaching the handleless door, Frank gave a tentative push and it swung open. Warily he stepped inside and blinked for a moment in the darkness.

"Joe! Quick!"

A man lay huddled on a cot. His face and the blanket he clutched were smeared with dried blood, and he moaned and heaved for breath.

"The man's unconscious," said Frank as he took the limp wrist for a pulse. "Find water, Joe. Maybe there's some in the jug on the table."

Joe looked into the container. "We're in luck!" He soaked his handkerchief and bathed the injured man's face. As the blood and dirt came away, the boy gave a gasp of surprise.

Hank Sutton!

"He's badly hurt," Frank observed. "Cuts and bruises on the head, and shock. Might be fractures, too,"

"I'll call the police ambulance," Joe volunteered. "We passed a house about a mile down the road. They must have a phone."

"Hurry!" Frank urged. "I'll stay here."

Joe sprinted for his motorcycle. While he was gone, Frank searched the dim hut for clues to an assailant, but found nothing.

Soon an ambulance, its red lights blinking, was speeding toward Shantytown. A police car followed. When they passed the house where Joe had telephoned, he zoomed after them.

At Shantytown he led an intern and two stretcher-bearers across the sand to the hut where Frank waited with the injured Sutton.

"How is he?" asked the doctor quickly on entering. "Is he conscious yet?"

"No, he's delirious," Frank said. "He keeps mumbling something over and over—a man's name."

"Whose?" asked Joe eagerly. He had appeared in the doorway, with Chief Collig behind him.

Frank looked up at them with a frown. "Alf Lundborg's, I'm afraid."

"So he took his revenge on Sutton," the chief concluded. "That's bad."

The intern hustled everyone out of the way. Expertly the injured man was transferred to the stretcher and borne across the sand to the waiting ambulance.

Chief Collig and the boys trailed along. "We'll have to pick up Alf," the chief remarked. "He had the perfect motive for assaulting Sutton."

"Just the same I don't believe he did it," Joe declared stoutly.

"Sorry, fellows," the chief said regretfully as they reached the road, "but regardless of the suspicions against Sutton, I have no choice."

Frank and Joe walked sadly back to the pine grove, mounted their motorcycles, and rode home. They ate lunch quietly, puzzling over the case.

"What now?" Joe asked glumly. "All we did this morning was to get Alf in trouble."

"Great detectives we are!" said Frank, disgusted. "How about walking downtown? I have another idea."

"About what?"

"The Fizzle soda. Since the person who had a bottle of it was in our boat—the bald fellow or someone else—he was in Bayport. Maybe he did buy some here."

The two set off and strode briskly along the sidewalk. At the first grocery store they turned in. "Do you carry Fizzle soda?" Frank asked.

"No, I don't."

The young detectives went into all the drugstores, markets, and lunch counters along their way. Always they asked the same question, and received the same answer. Nobody sold Fizzle soda.

At last they entered a downtown sweetshop which was a meeting place for many of their friends. "Hi!" called Tony Prito from a booth where he was seated with Jerry Gilroy.

"Hello, fellows," Frank greeted them. "We'll be over in a minute."

Meanwhile, he asked the soda clerk about Fizzle, but received a negative answer. "Only place I've ever seen it anywhere around these parts is Northport. I live near there."

Northport again!

Frank and Joe walked over to their friends. "Any news of Chet and Biff?" Tony asked.

"Nothing but a postcard," Frank answered.

"What do you think really happened to them?" Jerry asked worriedly. "Did they go off on a mission of their own? Or *were* they kidnaped?"

"We don't know," Frank confessed. "But there haven't been any ransom notes."

"It's dull around here without the fellows." Tony sighed. "We were going on a nice camping trip."

"Chet and Biff told us about it," said Joe. "Frank and I have an idea maybe they're being hidden on one of the coast islands."

"Could be," Tony said. "I remember Biff mentioned Hermit Island—the one owned by a queer old recluse who lives on it."

"He mentioned that to us, too," Joe recalled. "I wonder if that old man has seen any sign of Chet and Biff?"

"Say!" Tony's face suddenly lighted up. "Why don't we get your boat and go out for a look at

Hermit Island? It's early enough yet. How about it?"

"Good idea!" Jerry exclaimed.

"Right!" Frank said enthusiastically.

Joe was already on his feet. "Come on! Let's go!" To Frank he said, "The mystery of Mr. French's mix-up last night can wait."

Jerry and Tony paid for their ice cream, and the four hurried out to Jerry's car. A short drive brought them to the Hardy boathouse.

"Let's take both our boats," Tony proposed. "We might need them—if we find Chet and Biff."

They piled into the *Sleuth* and Frank steered the craft down to the dock where Tony kept the *Napoli*. Just as the two boats were ready to cast off, Callie Shaw and Iola Morton walked out onto Tony's dock.

"Oh, are you boys going for a ride?" Callie asked. "May we come along?"

"Gosh, Callie," Frank said doubtfully, "this isn't exactly a pleasure cruise. We're bound for Hermit Island to look for Chet and Biff."

"Oh, then you have to take us," pleaded Iola. "After all, Chet's my brother." Her eyes filled with tears. "Please, Frank."

"Iola's right," Joe agreed. "The girls want to find Chet and Biff as much as we do."

"Okay," said Frank. "Pile in, then!" Iola cheered up at once and the Hardys helped the girls into the stern of the *Sleuth*.

The boats moved swiftly out the harbor, with Frank leading the way in the slightly faster *Sleuth.* Before long, the shore islands came into sight, with their white, drifted sand, scrubby vegetation, and huge, barren rocks.

Hermit Island, a big craggy pile, loomed out of the water higher than all the others. It was attractive but wild looking.

"Too rough on this side to land," Frank called over to the *Napoli.* "Good beach on the lee shore, though, I believe. Follow me!"

The search party rounded the island. After the girls had stepped onto firm sand, the four boys tied their mooring ropes to trees at the edge of the beach. All went ashore and gazed at the lonely spot.

"This is a spooky place," commented Iola, looking around her uneasily.

"It does give one the creeps," Callie agreed.

The boys laughed but felt they should proceed carefully. With Frank and Joe in the lead, they set off on a faint path that wound along the shore at the base of the steep, rocky hill which formed the heart of the island. Above the searchers loomed jagged cliffs, cut here and there by deep ravines, thick with pines and coarse grass.

At times Joe cupped his hands and shouted, "Hallooo . . . Bi-iff . . . Che-e-t!"

There was no answer. "Looks hopeless," Joe commented.

At last the path began to rise steeply. The four boys moved upward much faster than Iola and Callie. Finally the girls dropped behind. The boys continued on, clambering and puffing, forgetful of everything but the tough terrain they were fighting.

Suddenly a sharp scream rang out from below. "Callie!" cried Frank, whirling.

CHAPTER XIII

The Threatening Figure

TUMBLING and sliding, the four boys rushed pell-mell down the steep path to Iola and Callie. The girls clung together in fright.

"What is it, Callie?" cried Frank.

Speechless, the girl pointed upward. From the top of the bluff a wild-looking old man with a long, dirty white beard was pointing a shotgun at them.

His clothes were torn, and he wore a battered felt hat. The weird figure stood motionless, silhouetted against the blue sky. The afternoon sunlight gleamed on the barrels of his weapon.

"He must be the hermit," muttered Joe.

"Git off my island!" came the strong, deep voice of the old man. The shotgun jerked threateningly. "Git, I say!"

"We'd better do as he says," Frank advised.

He took Callie's arm. Joe grabbed Iola's. The six young people scooted for the beach.

As they followed the path, the Hardys and their friends could see the strange man darting from rock to rock along the top of the bluff above them. He did not let them out of his sight. When they reached the boats, Frank and Joe quickly helped the girls safely aboard the *Sleuth*.

Joe took the wheel while Frank cast off. The *Sleuth* and the *Napoli* were run just out of shotgun range, then throttled down while their passengers took another look at their adversary. The

old man stood in the same threatening attitude on the hilltop.

"You know," Frank noted, "for an old fellow he has a powerful voice."

"He's plenty spry, too," Joe added. "Did you see how he jumped across those rocks? He's nimble as a goat!"

"And did you notice his shotgun?" Frank asked. "It was very well cared for; not like his beard and clothes!"

"There was no nonsense about that gun," Joe agreed. "I'd like to know what the man's trying to keep us away from!"

"Maybe he just wants to be left alone," Callie suggested.

"After all, he is a hermit," added Iola.

"Whatever he is," declared Joe, "I'd like to get a closer look at him sometime."

Joe put on power and the *Sleuth* shot forward over the water. The *Napoli* trailed close behind.

As the island dropped astern, Frank remarked, "I can still make out the hermit. He's standing motionless on that hilltop."

The two speedboats crossed the wide expanse of Bayport harbor and came to rest at Tony's dock.

"Say, you fellows don't have any transportation down here," Jerry recalled. "Shall I pick you up at your boathouse?"

"No, thanks," Frank replied. "Joe and I came

out to do some sleuthing. We'll walk. We have a few stops to make."

"Okay, we'll give Iola and Callie a lift, then." They helped the girls ashore and Frank and Joe waved good-by.

After locking the *Sleuth* in her berth, Frank and Joe walked to the center of town. "Let's stop at headquarters," Frank suggested as they approached the familiar stone building. "Maybe there's some new word on Sutton."

The boys found Chief Collig in conference with Lieutenant Daley.

"It's all right. Come in, fellows," the chief invited. "Daley's been over at the hospital. Sutton has regained consciousness."

"What did he say?" Frank inquired eagerly.

"He claims he doesn't know who beat him up," replied Lieutenant Daley. "Says he was hit from behind and never saw his attacker."

"But that can't be true!" Frank protested. "The bruises I saw were mostly on his face."

"Oh, he knows who did it, all right," Lieutenant Daley agreed. "Only he's covering up for somebody. Why should he try to protect that big fellow he tried to frame last night?"

"How about Alf?" Joe broke in. "What's his story?"

"We have Lundborg in a cell," Lieutenant Daley answered. "Of course he denies any part in the beating."

"We can't hold him much longer," put in Chief Collig. "There's no evidence against him."

"Of course not! Alf wouldn't beat up a fellow half his size," Joe declared.

"Then why did Sutton mumble Lundborg's name in his delirium?" the chief countered.

"Sutton had a grudge against Alf. It must have been on his mind," Frank suggested.

"That could be," Chief Collig conceded. "How have you two boys been making out? Any new clues on Chet or Biff? We have none."

"No, we haven't," Frank answered. "We went out to Hermit Island on a hunch this afternoon, but had no luck there, either."

"Do you know anything about that hermit, Chief?" Joe inquired.

"A little," the chief returned. "Remember him, Daley? Queer old bird. Somebody left him the whole island in a will. He said it was just the place he wanted, to get away from the crazy world!"

"Yes." The tall lieutenant chuckled. "He moved out there for good some years ago. Never let anybody land on his island."

"We found that out. He chased us off pretty fast this afternoon," Joe said.

"Wha-a-t?" drawled the lieutenant, turning for a good look at the boy.

"Who are you kidding?" Chief Collig grinned.

"What's so funny?" Joe asked. "He threatened us with a shotgun."

"That's impossible," Chief Collig said flatly. "He's dead!"

Frank and Joe looked at each other in astonishment. "Then he's a mighty spry dead man," Joe declared.

Chief Collig shook his head. "The hermit died last fall and the Coast Guard brought him back to the mainland for burial. He had no one to leave the island to, so it belongs to the state."

"Wow!" Joe cried out. "Then the man we saw isn't the real hermit and had no right to order us off."

"Right," Chief Collig agreed. "It's state property. Anyone can go there. My jurisdiction doesn't cover it. Report this man to the Coast Guard."

"We will, if he bothers us again," Frank stated.

After leaving the police station, the young detectives walked along Bayport's main street toward Mr. French's costume store.

"That phony hermit wasn't joking," Frank said. "He wanted us off the island and no fooling. What do you think he's up to?"

Joe stopped short and said excitedly, "What if Chet and Biff were taken to Hermit Island?"

"Then this faker might know about the kidnaping. Is he in on the game, too?"

"The old guy could be holding them prisoner," Joe went on. "That's why he chased us away! He didn't dare risk having us looking around."

"Hermit Island isn't very far away from Shantytown," Frank said. "The rubber mask we found could have floated out from one place as well as from the other, depending on the tide."

"But how about the pieces of the boys' costumes the police found among the shacks?" Joe asked, perplexed. "How do they fit in with the Hermit Island theory?"

"Chet and Biff could've been transported to the island from Shantytown," reasoned Frank.

As he spoke, the brothers came to the costume shop. "I hope Mr. French is here," Frank said. "We'll ask him why he—"

The boys suddenly gasped and stared in amazement at the big display window of the store. In it were a gorilla and a magician costume!

"The same kind of suits we were wearing the night Biff and Chet disappeared!" Frank cried out.

"Yes," Joe agreed in high excitement. "And that was the night of the bank robbery!"

CHAPTER XIV

Signal Three

"THERE's something queer about this costume store," Frank said positively. "Maybe the bank robbers got their masks here!"

"And Mr. French came to our house in the middle of the night to tell us about it, then lost his nerve," Joe added.

"Why are the same costumes in this window as those we wore?" Frank wondered. "Are they a signal to somebody?"

"There's one way to find out," Joe replied. "We'll ask Mr. French himself." He pushed the heavy glass door.

It was locked. Peering inside the store, the boys saw that it was deserted. A shaft of light from the back room pierced the late-afternoon shadows within. Joe banged on the heavy glass with his knuckles but no one came.

"Let's try the back entrance," Frank muttered.

An alley separated the costume store from the next building. The boys slipped along this cobbled passageway to a dingy yard behind the shop. Quietly they stepped up to the rear door. Voices could be heard inside.

As Joe raised his fist to knock, Frank grabbed his arm. "Wait! Listen!"

A man's voice droned on indistinguishably, then snapped out a single, sharp word.

"Kidnap!"

Breathless, Frank and Joe strained to hear more.

"You fools!" said a new voice derisively.

A third speaker broke in harshly. The phrase "no second mistake" rasped out clearly.

". . . signal three . . ." came another snatch.

The Hardys listened intently but were unable to catch any more of the conversation.

Silently Frank beckoned Joe into the alley. "I have a hunch!" he said. "Chet was wearing a gorilla suit just like mine. What if he and Biff were kidnaped in place of you and me?"

Joe's eyes widened with excitement. "Then the kidnapers are the bank robbers—and they would still be out to get us!" he exclaimed. "That's what they meant by 'no second mistake'!"

Frank nodded. "They're probably holding Chet and Biff because they're afraid to let them go!"

"But why were they after us in the first place?" Joe asked, puzzled.

"I don't know," Frank admitted. "But I have a plan. Come on! We must act fast!"

The boys ran from the alley and hailed a passing taxi. When they reached home, the brothers found that their father had just returned and was in his study. Fenton Hardy listened in concern and amazement to his sons' discovery.

"How I'd like to pick up those thugs and question them!" he exclaimed. "But that would only tip them off."

"And we haven't enough evidence to hold them," Frank added.

Mr. Hardy frowned. "The best we can do is put a police tail on them and hope to find out more that way." He reached for the phone.

"Wait, Dad!" Frank pleaded. "I have a scheme. Joe and I will go back to the shop. We'll *let* them kidnap us. Then Collig's men will really have something on the gang and can nab them."

"I don't know," their father considered. "It's plenty risky."

"Please, Dad," Joe urged. "The faster we crack the case, the sooner we'll find Chet and Biff."

Fenton Hardy was concerned for his sons' safety, but was proud of their willingness to risk capture for the sake of their missing chums.

"All right," he agreed. "I'll alert the police. We'll station ourselves outside the store. As soon as the gang tries to take you away, we'll close in!"

"Good," said Frank, satisfied.

As their father dialed headquarters, he checked his watch and said to Frank and Joe, "Give Collig and me twenty minutes from now to get set. Then go into the store."

The boys sped downtown on their motorcycles, parked near the costume shop, and slipped down the alley. The men were still talking inside the back room of the store. The brothers waited, eyes fixed on their wrist watches.

"Now!" Frank whispered at last. "Let's take the chance that 'signal three' means knock three times!"

The boys walked to the back door and Frank gave three hard raps.

Immediately the voices became silent. A lock clicked and the door swung a few inches inward. A man's face peered out at the boys. He was the speedboat pilot with the slicked-back hair—the one Mr. Caine had identified as Ben Stark!

Frank and Joe gave no sign of recognition. Stark's eyes, however, widened in astonishment.

"I know the store is closed," Frank said to him, "but we need something desperately. We're the Hardy boys. May we come in?"

Stark's expression changed from amazement to oily politeness. "Of course, boys!" he answered, and swung the door wide. "Come right inside!"

Frank and Joe passed into a dim storeroom, lighted by a single bulb overhead. On one side, two tough-looking men they had never seen before eyed them in stunned silence. Ben Stark closed the door and stood with his back against it.

"So you are the famous Hardy boys!" he said, smiling widely. "Of course I've heard of you, but I don't think we've met before."

Stark looked hard at them, but the boys' expressions betrayed nothing. He indicated his companions. "This is Mr. Moran and Mr. Duke," he said. Moran nodded. Duke, a lanky, pale-faced man, merely stared.

"Haven't I heard that you've been working on a new case?" Stark asked. "What do you suppose has happened to your missing friends?"

Recognizing the attempt to pump them, the young sleuths played along.

"They must have drowned," Frank replied sadly. He made no reference to the postcard in Chet's handwriting.

For a moment Stark looked puzzled. Then he said with exaggerated sympathy, "Isn't it strange there's been so much excitement in town lately? Even a bank robbery!"

"That won't be a mystery for long," Frank boasted to test the man's reaction. "My father, Fenton Hardy, has it practically solved. The robbers had better watch out!"

Ben Stark's oily smile faded. He looked hard

at his two companions by the wall. Catching the signal, the men left their places and casually drew nearer to Frank and Joe. Both boys sensed the coming attack and summoned all their will power to appear nonchalant.

"By the way, where's Mr. French?" Joe asked, glancing casually around the room. There was no answer.

The next instant the three men lunged forward and leaped on the brothers!

Boxes tumbled from shelves in the struggle, and the single light bulb swung crazily from the ceiling. Frank pretended to be fighting off his assailants, but finally he allowed his arms to be pinioned.

Joe, meanwhile, had been thrown against a bank of shelves and had fallen to the floor as though stunned. Panting, the men quickly bound, gagged, and blindfolded the two young detectives.

"Now," gloated Stark, "if your old man and the police don't call off the hunt for the bank robbers, they'll never see you again!"

Frank and Joe listened intently, hoping to learn more, but the men said nothing further.

A door slammed. There was a short, silent wait. Then they heard a car engine running in the yard behind the store.

"Okay!" came Stark's voice. "Coast is clear!"

Frank and Joe were lifted up, carried a little

way, then dropped on the floor of the automobile.

Tensely the two boys waited to hear police whistles and Chief Collig barking orders. But the car began to move, rolling swiftly out the alley, and away.

"What happened to our plan?" Frank wondered. "Where's Dad?"

"We must have gone in too soon," Joe thought, dismayed. "The police couldn't get here in time!"

As the car drove on, Frank and Joe recognized the sounds of heavy traffic all around them. Gradually the vehicle picked up speed. The engine purred steadily, and the tires whined along on what could only be open highway.

Presently the car swerved, bumped over uneven ground a short distance, and stopped. In the sudden silence the blindfolded youths could hear the sound of surf on the beach.

"We're near the shore," Frank reasoned. "Shantytown perhaps. The time it took getting here seems about the same as when we came before."

The car doors were opened. Again the boys were lifted and carried. A minute later each of them felt a jarring pain as he was dropped on a wooden floor. Rough hands ripped away their blindfolds.

Although tightly bound, the Hardys struggled to sitting positions. They were in a small board shack. A little light came through a tiny window high up in one of the walls.

Ben Stark and Moran were going out the door. Stark looked back. "Keep your eyes open, Duke," he ordered sharply. "Those kids are slippery."

"Don't worry," the pale-faced man replied insolently.

After his two companions had left, he went to a water bucket in one corner, dipped in a tin cup, and drank thirstily. Then he sat down in a wooden chair and tilted back lazily against the wall.

Frank and Joe listened anxiously for sounds of rescue. They could hear the sea, but nothing else.

Carefully they looked over their prison. The shack was crudely built out of broken crates and old two-by-fours. Long, sharp points of nails stuck through the wall near Duke's chair. At the rear of the room was a little squat wood-burning stove.

Cramped and helpless, the boys could only wait. As night came on, Duke stood up and lighted a kerosene lantern hanging on the wall. Then he sat down and tilted back his chair again.

"Might as well face it," thought Frank. "Rescue isn't coming." He looked at Joe with silent urgency, and his eyes said plainly, "It's up to us!"

CHAPTER XV

Outwitting a Suspect

ALTHOUGH bound and gagged, the Hardys exchanged messages. Frank's glance slid to their guard, tilted back in his chair against the wall. Then he looked at his brother.

Joe nodded slightly to show he understood and looked toward the lantern. The glass was turning black with soot and the room was in deep shadow.

"Lucky it's dark in here," he thought, "because we'll have to get these ropes off without being seen."

Frank's eyes fastened on the long nails he had seen sticking through the wall near the chair legs. If only he could get his back to those sharp points!

Cautiously he inched toward the wall. Duke, who appeared to be asleep, did not stir. Joe also moved. Bit by bit, the brothers worked their way closer to the protruding nails.

At last Frank sat with his back against the wall,

not far from the guard's chair. Hardly daring to breathe, he felt behind him until a tenpenny spike pricked his wrist. If he was lucky, his scheme would work!

Frank eyed his captor. The man was still asleep. Quickly Frank rubbed the rope against the sharp point. He could feel the strands separate, one at a time. His arms and back ached, but he kept on doggedly.

Finally the rope was severed. His hands freed, he removed the gag, then pulled out his pocket-knife and cut the ropes around his ankles. Reaching over, he cut Joe's bonds.

Then Frank seized a leg of Duke's tilted chair and jerked it out from under the guard. *Slam!* Duke fell on his back and cried out.

Frank and Joe leaped on him together, but he rolled away. As he bounced to his feet, Joe brought him down with a tackle.

Fighting desperately, the guard kicked, bit, scratched, and finally broke away. Gasping, he backed into a corner. As Frank went after him, Duke grabbed the kerosene lantern and hurled it. The boys ducked.

Crash! The glass shattered and kerosene drenched the opposite wall. A flame licked up the side of the shack.

"Water!" Joe yelled. "The bucket!"

He tore off his shirt and tried to beat out the flames. At the same time, Frank and Duke grappled for the pail. Duke jerked it away and flung it at Joe. The bucket narrowly missed him, slamming against the wall. The water splashed over onto the flames with a hissing sound.

"You young fools! I'll get you for this!" Duke picked up the chair and raised it over his head. But Frank swung a right-hand haymaker. It caught Duke in the solar plexus and he went down in a heap.

"He's out cold!" Joe cried, whipped off his shirt, and finally smothered the flames. "What a sock that was!"

Duke moaned and stirred. Swiftly the boys felt around until they found the cut ropes. Panting, they bound their prisoner's hands and feet.

"That should hold him," said Joe as the boys stood up.

"Now, let's see where we are," Frank suggested.

Cautiously he opened the shack door and the brothers slipped outside.

"It's the edge of Shantytown," Joe whispered after a quick look around.

Across a whitish stretch of sand they could see the dark shacks and beyond them a red glare from beach fires. A nearly full moon sailed in and out of heavy clouds.

Suddenly a figure detached itself from the shadow of the shanties and glided quickly across the sand toward them. Fists ready, Frank and Joe set themselves for a fight!

"Put up your hands!" came a firm command. "You're under arrest!"

At the same moment, moonlight fell upon a familiar face. "Pat Muster!" Frank exclaimed joyfully. "Are we glad to see you!"

Pat Muster was a plain-clothes man on the Bayport police force. The brawny, red-haired man turned his flashlight on the bruised, disheveled boys. "So you fought your way out, eh?" he said, putting away his revolver. "Too bad you didn't yell for help. My men and I were staked out by the shacks, keeping an eye on this place."

Frank grinned ruefully. "I wish we'd known that. We didn't call out, because we were afraid of bringing more of the gang."

"Where's our father?" Joe asked.

"He took a squad of police and followed Stark and the other fellow. The chief went back to headquarters."

"I see," said Frank. "When you didn't close in at the store, we thought the plan had backfired."

"Your father suggested that we follow you, on the chance of locating the rest of the gang. Sorry I left you in the shack so long," he added. "I was hoping some more of these tough birds would turn up and we'd make a bigger haul."

"We have one of them for you," Joe said, "all trussed up and ready to go."

Pat Muster chuckled. "I've got to hand it to

you, boys," he said. "You always deliver the goods!"

He turned toward the shanties and gave a low whistle. Here and there a half dozen figures appeared from the shadows and crossed to join the boys and Muster at the shack.

"Wait here," the officer ordered his men. He and the Hardys entered the shanty. The detective beamed his flashlight on the prone figure of Duke, who blinked and scowled.

"Now that you're awake," Frank said, "you'd be smart to tell us where our missing chums are."

The man glared and did not answer.

"Don't waste time on him," Joe advised. "Let's search this place. Maybe the bank loot is hidden here."

Frank and Joe borrowed flashlights from two of the men outside and began to help Detective Muster. They inspected the crude walls and flooring. Finally, they stood up, disappointed.

"Nothing," Frank said, "and there's no other place to hide anything except in the little stove."

At this, Duke darted an apprehensive look at the stove. In two quick strides Frank reached it, lifted the stove lid, and plunged his hand inside.

"There's something here!" he exclaimed. He pulled out a limp object. "A rubber mask! I think there are more!" he added quickly, reaching in again. One after another, he brought out four additional false faces.

Joe whistled. "The bank robbers' masks! What a find! This shack must have been their headquarters—for a time, at least!"

"Great work, Frank!" Detective Muster congratulated him. "There'll probably be plenty of fingerprints on those masks." He pulled a large folded paper sack from his pocket and opened it. "Drop them in here."

The detective summoned two of his men to unbind the prisoner. Then they handcuffed Duke and led him to the police cars hidden in the pines on the other side of Shore Road. Muster and the boys followed. When they reached headquarters, Chief Collig sent the rubber masks to his lab for immediate fingerprint analysis. Finally he turned to the Hardys. "Letting yourselves be kidnaped was a daring stunt, boys. But you got results." He looked at Duke, who sat beside him, scowling.

Frank drew the chief aside and asked quietly, "How about Dad and his men? Have they located Chet and Biff?"

The chief shook his head. "They should have radioed in by now," he replied. "Let's see what we can get out of the prisoner." He walked over and stood in front of Duke. "If you know what's good for you—" he began but was interrupted by a clatter of feet outside.

The next moment Ben Stark and Moran, handcuffed together, entered the chief's office, followed by Fenton Hardy and two policemen.

"Dad!" cried Joe. "Did you find Chet and Biff?"

"No," said his father quietly. "Are you boys all right? You look as if you'd had a rough time."

"We're okay," Frank assured his father quickly. "Tell us your story."

"We followed Stark and Moran from Shantytown," his father explained. "They drove down to the docks and sat there, apparently waiting for a boat. When it didn't show up, they headed back to Shantytown. So did we. As soon as I saw that Pat was missing from his station, I knew you boys and your guard had been brought here. We arrested these two right in the shack."

"Do Stark and Moran know where Biff and Chet are?" Joe asked.

"I think they know all right," Fenton Hardy said grimly. "But they're not talking."

Frank and Joe looked disappointed.

"Cheer up," Chief Collig advised them. "You've done a terrific job. We can hold these three on a charge of kidnaping you. After we've checked the prints on the masks you found, we'll probably be able to identify them conclusively as the bank robbers."

After the sullen prisoners were taken away, Frank and Joe told their father and the police what had happened to them. Then the Hardys left the station and piled into the detective's car.

"We'll pick up our motorcycles tomorrow," Frank said.

When they reached home, the three shared a late supper of cold chicken, milk, and apple pie. Then they went straight to bed.

The next morning, as the boys were coming downstairs to breakfast, the telephone rang. "I'll get it," said Mr. Hardy, picking up the receiver.

A few minutes later he joined the boys in the dining room. "That was Chief Collig," the detective announced. "The fingerprints of Ben Stark, Fritz Stark, Duke, and Moran—all wanted by the police—were on the masks. One set of prints is unidentified."

"They probably belong to the big bald fellow," said Frank. "The one Mr. Caine mentioned."

"Caine!" exclaimed their father. "In all the excitement I forgot to tell you that Mr. Caine phoned yesterday just after you left for the costume shop. He wants you to call him."

At this news the boys hurried to the hall and Frank dialed the long-distance call to Northport. In a few seconds Frank was speaking to the friendly dock manager.

"You remember those fellows who rented the *Black Cat* from me?" he asked. "Well, one of 'em left an empty envelope in his hotel room. I own the hotel, that's how I found it. Thought it might help you to track 'em down. Fritz Stark's address is on it."

"That's wonderful, Mr. Caine!" Frank cried out, and said to Joe, "He has what might be the Starks' address." Turning back to the telephone, Frank asked, "Where was the letter from?"

"Let me see . . ." the dock manager said. "It's from Worldwide Radio Distributors, Yokohama, over in Japan!"

CHAPTER XVI

Skeleton Symbol

"MR. CAINE," said Frank in a puzzled tone, "may I have the address on the letter?"

After jotting down the information, Frank thanked him and said good-by. He told Joe, "Just a San Francisco hotel. But the sender was the distributor for radios in Yokohama."

"Sutton had a Yokohama radio!" Joe exclaimed. "And we saw him talking to Ben Stark that day at Shantytown."

"The radio seems to be a connection between them," Frank pointed out. "I think we'd better go back to the hi-fi shop, and find out more about the identity of Yokohama Super-X purchasers."

After eating breakfast, the boys hurried off, first to pick up their motorcycles, then to go to the hi-fi shop. When they entered the store, the young clerk was glad to see them.

"Change your minds, fellows?" he asked hopefully. "Like to buy one of those sets?"

"We *would* like to look at them," Frank replied.

Immediately the clerk bustled off and returned with four of the compact little radios. "Go ahead," he invited. "Try them."

While Joe flicked the button on one set, the young man said, "These are neat. As I told you the other day, we buy them from a distributor in Japan." In response to Frank's query about who had purchased them, the clerk gave the customers' names, all familiar to the Hardys. None of them could be suspect.

"Three of these radios came in yesterday afternoon. I could give you boys a good price, since we bought them at a big discount."

"How come?" Frank asked.

"Well, we didn't buy these from the distributor," the clerk admitted. "These were brought in by a fellow who wanted to sell them at a secondhand price, even though they're brand new. My boss snapped up all three. He knows a bargain."

"I see." Frank nodded. "No questions asked."

"Oh, it's not anything illegal," the clerk hastened to say. "They were brought in by a respectable businessman, Mr. French, who owns the costume store down the street."

"Mr. French!" the boys echoed in amazement.

"Yes. What's so strange about that?"

"Oh, nothing, I guess," Frank replied. "You just reminded us that we must see Mr. French ourselves right away. The radios will have to wait. Come on, Joe!"

While the mystified clerk stared after the Hardys, they bolted from the shop and hurried along the sidewalk toward the costume shop.

"Mr. French again," Joe muttered, shaking his head. "Is he one of this gang?"

"Somehow I trust him," Frank replied. "Maybe the robbers are forcing him to play along with them, and have threatened harm to his family unless he does."

"He didn't look very happy the afternoon we picked up our costumes," Joe recalled. "Those men in his shop *were* threatening him. And when he came to our house in the middle of the night, it was no mistake!"

"He knows Dad's a detective," Frank said. "I think he wanted him and was confused when we answered the door."

"Well, we'll soon find out," Joe said as they neared the shop.

"It looks closed," Frank remarked. The heavy door was shut and the blinds drawn. Going closer, the boys saw a sign in the window:

Closed Indefinitely

"I wonder why," said Joe. "Has Mr. French gone out of business?"

"Hey," Frank cried out, "where are the gorilla and magician outfits that were in the window yesterday afternoon?"

Only one costume was now on display—a skeleton suit, which stood up with outspread arms, like a scarecrow!

"I hate to think what *that* costume means, if it's a signal," Joe said.

"Never mind," Frank said. "We must find Mr. French. Perhaps he lives over the store." Frank strode to a door at one side of the building. "Yes, here's his name on the bell plate."

Impatiently the young detective jabbed with his thumb at the button. The bell sounded loudly but no one answered.

"Hey!" came a sharp voice. "What are you two doing here?"

Frank and Joe whirled to face their two chums Jerry Gilroy and Tony Prito.

"We're sleuthing around," Joe replied, and grinned. "What are *you* fellows up to?"

Tony explained that he and Jerry were on an errand for Mr. Prito, then asked, "Have you found out anything more about Chet and Biff?"

"We found out plenty!" Joe exploded. "Chet and Biff were kidnaped by the bank robbers, who mistook them for Frank and me."

"What!" cried Tony and Jerry. While they listened intently, Frank and Joe gave the details of their adventure the night before.

"But where is the gang holding them?" Jerry wondered. "Could it be Hermit Island?"

"Could be," Frank said. "We found out the hermit we saw is a fake. The real one's dead."

"And when Dad trailed Stark and Moran last night," Joe put in, "they went to the dock and waited for a boat. That could mean the rest of the gang—and Chet and Biff—are some place only accessible by water."

"Then what are we waiting for?" urged Jerry. "Let's head for Hermit Island!"

"Yes—and no girls this time," Tony added. "That phony hermit carries a shotgun, and if the robbers are there, the danger is double."

"Right," Frank said. "We'd better take both boats, Tony. In case of trouble, we'll be able to split up, or help each other."

Tony agreed eagerly. "Then we'll meet you at your dock at one-thirty," Frank told him.

As their two friends hurried off, Frank and Joe walked to their motorcycles and rode home.

As they dismounted in front of their garage, Aunt Gertrude appeared behind the back screen door, wringing her hands nervously.

"Hi, Auntie!" Joe called cheerfully. "Where are Mother and Dad?"

"Your mother has gone shopping and your father's off on some more detective work! There's a giant in the living room waiting for *you*."

"A what?" Joe asked, entering the house.

Aunt Gertrude made a sweeping motion with her arms. "A man," she said, "*a great big* man!"

Laughing, Frank led the way into the living room. This must be Alf Lundborg!

The visitor's huge frame certainly dwarfed the Hardys' furniture. Grinning, he shook each brother's hand in his crushing grip.

"I'm out of jail again," he told them. "Sutton wouldn't say I attacked him, so they finally let me go."

"I *knew* you didn't do it, Alf," said Joe.

The stevedore's good-natured face clouded. "No, I wouldn't touch a little weasel like Sutton," he agreed. "But it makes me sore to be accused of doing it! What I came to tell you, though, is this—I know who *did* beat him up. It was one of his own pals!"

"Ben Stark?" Frank asked curiously.

"No, a fellow they call Pops. Remember I told you about the bunch who were always fighting with one another? Well, Sutton and Pops do most of it. Pops finally gave it to him good, but Sutton won't tell the police."

"That must mean they're in something illegal together," Frank reasoned. "How about this Pops, Alf—is he an old man?"

"No. Although he's bald, he's younger than Sutton—bigger and stronger. Talks loud, too. I don't know why they call him Pops."

Frank and Joe looked at each other excitedly.

Both immediately thought of Ben Stark's pal who was still at large. Could Pops be the Fizzle soda drinker?

"Thanks for telling us, Alf," said Joe. "We're glad you're out of jail. You've been in twice and both times because of us."

"You couldn't help it," replied their big friend, "and you spoke up for me both times. I appreciate that."

After Alf had left, the brothers had some lunch, then headed for the waterfront on their motorcycles.

Tony and Jerry were already in the *Napoli* when the *Sleuth* came alongside the Prito dock. With serious, determined faces the four friends headed for Hermit Island.

As soon as they reached the ocean, the boys were confronted by a fast-darkening sky and choppy sea. With incredible swiftness, black clouds, with chains of lightning snapping underneath them, moved in from the south. Large raindrops began to pelt the boys. In another moment the darkness closed around them like nightfall. Lightning flashed on the heaving ocean and the rain smacked down on them almost painfully.

"Why didn't we bring slickers!" Joe exclaimed.

Through it all, Joe kept the *Sleuth*'s nose pointed northward. Presently, illuminated by the lightning, a rocky mass came into view.

"There's the island," Frank called out. "A motorboat's just pulling away, Joe!"

"Let's chase it!" Joe cried. "Some of the gang may be aboard and are escaping."

"Not now," Frank cautioned. "Chet and Biff come first!" As the boys watched, the dark-brown craft disappeared in the distance.

As suddenly as it had come up, the black squall passed over. The *Sleuth* and the *Napoli* circled toward the island's beach. By this time the rain had stopped.

The clouds parted, blue sky appeared, and the sun beat down again. Under its burning heat the boys' clothes began to dry out.

"The storm's probably driven that phony hermit under cover," Joe said. "Let's get ashore before he spots us."

The boys found a small cove fringed with small, scrubby oak trees. Quickly concealing their boats in this cover, they debarked and set out on the path around the island.

This time no one disturbed them. The trail climbed and then dropped down to the level of the shore again. Overhead loomed the wet bluff.

Suddenly Frank stopped and pointed to a dark opening in the gray rock ahead. "A cave!" he said quietly.

The boys crept nearer. Just outside the cave's entrance, Frank lifted a warning hand.

"Voices!" he whispered.

CHAPTER XVII

Hermit's Hideout

HOLDING themselves rigid against the damp rock, the four boys strained to listen. Somewhere inside the cave a man was talking rapidly, but his words were muffled and indistinct.

"What's he saying?" whispered Tony.

Frank motioned for the others to hold their places. Then he lay on his stomach and inched cautiously forward until his head was just outside the cave opening. From this position he could hear what was going on inside.

"Well, what's happening?" Jerry whispered impatiently. "Tug at his ankle, Joe!"

But just then Frank came wriggling backward. He jumped to his feet, and clutching his sides, hastened some distance down the path.

Joe, Tony, and Jerry ran after him.

"Frank—what's the matter?" his brother asked. "What was he saying?"

Frank tried to speak, but his chest heaved with

Frank could hear what was going on inside

suppressed laughter. Finally he managed to tell them: "The fellow was saying . . . 'B-buy B-b-butterfly Baby Foods'!"

"Wha-a-t!" The three boys looked at one another, completely mystified.

"We were listening to a radio," Frank blurted out. "The announcer was giving a commercial!"

"You mean the hermit's in there, listening to the radio?" Joe asked.

"I couldn't see," Frank replied. "Maybe Chet and Biff are there! It's likely, anyhow, that their guard went in to avoid the rain. Now that it's over, he'll probably come out again. Our best move is to find a good spot to lie in wait for him."

Near the cave mouth the boys found a large, brush-protected boulder and hid themselves behind it. For some time they waited. From inside the cave, snatches of music alternated with the announcer's voice.

At last Joe could stand it no longer. "Maybe there's nobody inside!" he burst out impatiently. "I'm going to have a look!"

"Careful!" Frank whispered, as his brother slipped out of hiding.

Joe darted to the path, lay down, and inched himself forward until he could see into the cavern. For several minutes he peered inside, then scrambled back behind the boulder.

"Somebody *is* in there!" he reported. "He's asleep and forgot to turn off his radio."

"Any sign of Chet and Biff?" Frank asked.

Joe shook his head. "No."

"Do you think it's the hermit?" Jerry asked.

"I don't know," Joe replied. "Anyway, he's alone."

"We could surprise this fellow while he's asleep," Tony said.

Frank nodded. "But Chet and Biff may be somewhere else on the island. Let's search while the fellow in the cave is asleep."

"Good idea," Joe agreed. "Look for a hut or shelter where the boys might be prisoners."

A brief examination of the gray bluff revealed a narrow cleft leading to the top of the precipice. Joe, ascending first, found himself on another path which seemed to rim the island from the top of the bluffs.

"Here's the trail the hermit used to keep us in sight yesterday," he told the others.

After scrambling up, Frank, Tony, and Jerry paused for a look about. Below them sparkled the bright ocean, extending to the mainland a few miles away. Behind lay a little plateau, overgrown with small pines and scrub oaks. In the center of the flat area rose a steep, rocky hill which gave the island its humping silhouette.

"A hut would be easy to camouflage among those trees," Frank remarked. "We'll have to spread out and comb every foot of the woods."

Though the youths worked carefully around

the plateau, they found no sign of any shelter. On the island's seaward side, where the growth was sparse, the boys checked the sides of the steep hill for caves. They saw none.

"It doesn't look very hopeful," Joe said at last. "If Biff and Chet were brought here, they've probably been carried off by now."

"The robbers might still be using this place," Jerry insisted. "It's a perfect hideout."

"They could have come here with the loot from the bank," Tony added, "and used the phony hermit to scare off intruders."

"Perhaps the gang is using the island merely as a stopping-off place," Frank suggested. "With this hill right in the middle, a lookout could spot boats approaching from miles away."

"Of course!" Joe took him up eagerly. "That's how the hermit happened to be waiting for us yesterday. Today is different. Don't forget that boat we saw pulling away. Chet and Biff may have been put aboard!"

"Right," said Joe. "Let's climb to the top of the hill and determine how far we *can* see."

Sparked by the new idea, the four boys attacked the steep hill at the center of the island. They worked their way among the rocks and pulled themselves upward by means of the short, tough brush.

"What a rough climb!" Jerry gasped.

As they climbed higher, the vegetation became too flimsy to use as support, and the hill's cone became even steeper. Still the boys pressed upward, panting, with Frank in the lead. Finally he clambered onto a flat, wind-swept area at the top—about twenty feet across—and threw himself down to rest.

Joe's head popped into view over the edge, and then Jerry's. Suddenly, from below them, came a sharp cry.

"Tony!" yelled Joe and Jerry together.

Sitting up, Frank saw a cloud of dust and stones tumbling and bouncing down the hill. A whole section of ground slid like a carpet along the steep slope, with Tony in the middle of it!

Frank, Joe, and Jerry slid in pursuit, bracing their feet hard against the slope like skiers!

Partly covered by loose earth, Tony Prito lay on his back where the hillside leveled off. He grinned up weakly at his three chums.

"You okay, Tony?" Joe cried anxiously.

"Think so. Can't seem to get up, though."

"Where are you hurt?" Frank asked.

"Ankle," Tony answered, rising to one knee.

Immediately a wince of pain crossed his face and he sank back again. Quickly Frank and Joe lifted their comrade to a standing position.

"Try now, Tony," Jerry urged. "Put just a little weight on it."

Though Tony's left leg appeared sturdy enough, the right one buckled at any pressure.

"It might be a fracture," Frank said. "We'll get you to a doctor, Tony."

While Jerry steadied the injured boy, Frank and Joe made a chair for him by interlocking their hands. Then they lifted Tony, who braced himself with one arm across each brother's shoulder.

Slowly the little procession made its way down to the level of the plateau. Moving more rapidly now, they followed the path around to the mainland side of the island.

Once among the scrub oaks and pines, the trail became too narrow for three persons to move abreast. Frank and Joe had to kick their way through the brush on each side as they advanced.

When they neared the beach at last, a small pine clump hindered Frank's progress. He kicked out determinedly.

"Hey, what's that?" cried Tony from his perch.

A dark garment, struck by Frank's foot, flopped into the path!

"A sailor's pea jacket," Jerry reported, stooping down. "And here are some more, under this pine brush."

"Pea jackets?" Frank exclaimed. "That's what the bank robbers wore!"

CHAPTER XVIII

Hidden Watchers

"THE bandits have been here!" Frank exclaimed. "Fellows, we're on the right track after all!"

"Wait till Chief Collig sees these pea jackets!" Joe exulted. "Pick 'em up, Jerry. Boy, what a bundle of clues!"

Jerry gathered the five bulky, damp jackets in his arms and staggered forward. Almost immediately a low-hanging oak branch snagged one of the coats and pulled it from his grasp.

"We'll never get to the boats at this rate," he despaired.

Frank, however, was more interested at this moment in the number of jackets. "There were only four robbers," he pointed out. "Who wore the fifth coat?"

"The driver of the getaway car, probably," Joe said. "Here, Jerry! We'll put Tony down for a minute. Why don't each of us put on a coat and you can carry the other one. That'll make it easier."

Swiftly the boys donned the jackets. Now Jerry moved ahead without difficulty, and the Hardys followed with Tony as fast as they could.

When they reached the top of the bluff that overlooked the cove where the boats lay hidden, the party paused for breath. Here was a fresh obstacle! Tony had to be lowered down the steep slope to the level of the beach!

"We'll slide him down," Frank decided. "Joe, you stay just below Tony, and keep his injured ankle from striking anything. Jerry and I can make a sling of our belts and lower him from one level to another."

Slowly the injured boy was brought from foothold to foothold, down to the sand. When they reached the boats, Tony's face was drawn and pale.

"Gosh, Tony—did we bump you too much coming down?" Frank asked solicitously.

"No, it's not your fault, fellows," their friend protested bravely. "My ankle's just starting to throb a little."

"Swelling, too," Frank noted with a frown. "Here, Joe, let's get him into the *Sleuth*. I'll head it for the Coast Guard dock as fast as I can. You and Jerry follow in the *Napoli*."

In another moment the *Sleuth's* powerful engine roared to life. Hastily stripping off the pea jacket, Frank bent over the wheel. Tony sat beside him, suffering in silence. The sleek craft sped across open water toward Bayport.

Meanwhile, Joe and Jerry threw the other pea jackets into the *Napoli*. Starting her engine, Joe piloted the slower speedboat out of the cove and along the island shore.

"Joe!" Jerry pointed to a boat coming around the island toward them.

"Oh, boy, this is trouble!" Joe exclaimed. "Hang on!"

He brought the wheel around hard. The *Napoli* swerved and ran in straight toward shore.

Jerry gasped. "You're running aground!"

Joe did not answer. He had noticed a narrow fissure which cut through the bluffs, making a tiny V-shaped opening in the shoreline. He ran the *Napoli* straight into the small slot of water, crashing through low-growing brush at its edges.

"Quick, Jerry," he directed, shutting off the motor, "grab some of these pine branches and pull them down on top of us!"

Clutching the sticky, sweet-smelling limbs, the boys crouched low and waited. Soon the slow, regular throb of a boat's motor could be heard. The strange brown boat, carrying two men, came into view.

The craft seemed to move with maddening slowness. Luckily the two men in it kept looking forward. From his place of concealment, Joe studied them carefully. The one in the stern was a short, muscular fellow, whose shock of white-blond hair gleamed in the sunshine.

"Jerry," Joe hissed, "I've seen those guys before! They were in Mr. French's shop when we picked up our costumes!" He added in a whisper, "The blond one must be Fritz Stark. He looks just like Ben, except for the different-colored hair."

Jerry gripped Joe's arm. "He's standing up! He'll see us!"

But Fritz Stark pointed straight ahead of him and called out to the man at the wheel, "Nick, take her to the hidden inlet!"

The boys crouched tensely, watching the two men cruise slowly past them. When at last the dark-brown craft was out of sight, the boys took in deep breaths of relief. But the result was disastrous to Jerry.

"Kerchoo! Kerchoo!" The sounds echoed off the bluffs behind them and carried far over the water.

"Oh, golly, I'm sorry," Jerry whispered. "I'm allergic to pine."

"Sh! Keep down," Joe warned. "Maybe they heard you, and maybe they didn't."

With hearts pounding, the boys waited. The

gentle put-putting sound of the motorboat grew louder and faster, rising in crescendo to an angry roar.

"We're in for it," Joe groaned.

In another moment the prow of the brown boat knifed back into view. This time the men aboard scanned the shoreline suspiciously!

The boys clutched the pine branches in front of them. But it was no use. The *Napoli*'s hull was clearly visible to their pursuers.

"There they are!" Fritz Stark shouted. "In that boat!"

As the bandits' craft swerved sharply and ran straight up on the concealed boys, Joe whispered, "Run for it, Jerry!"

The thick-growing brush, which had helped to conceal them, now became an obstacle to their flight. Seizing the pithy branches, Joe pulled and squirmed until he could feel solid ground. But when he jumped up and walked, the thick growth clawed at his legs.

Thump! The robbers' boat crashed into the *Napoli*. Then the brush began to shake as the men fought their way toward the boys. "Grab them!" Stark yelled.

Jerry caught up to Joe and for an instant the boys hesitated. All around rose the gray, rocky bluffs. Just in front of them, however, was a narrow ravine which Joe had noticed earlier.

"Come on! I think we can make it!" Joe urged.

The boys scrambled madly uphill, their pursuers only yards behind! Hand over hand, they clambered upward. Once Jerry stumbled and Joe paused to help him regain his balance. The short, muscular Stark was now gaining rapidly.

Joe uprooted a small prickly bush and fired it back. The bush hit Stark in the face. He cried out in anger, but kept staggering upward. In a moment he made a leap for Joe's ankles!

"I've got you!" he cried as the boy slid backward on his stomach.

"Keep going, Jerry!" Joe shouted before turning to grapple with his antagonist.

At the same time the second man skirted them both, and disappeared over the top of the ravine, pursuing Jerry.

Though Joe fought savagely, Stark's weight finally won out and soon the boy's arms were pinned behind him and bound together with a belt.

Then Jerry appeared at the top of the ravine, his arms held securely by Stark's henchman. "Get down there!" his captor ordered roughly.

While he and the boy descended, Stark eyed Joe with an unpleasant smile.

"Hey, Nick," the blond man called, "look who's here!"

The henchman grinned as he recognized Joe. "One of the real Hardy boys!"

"What'll we do with him and his friend?"

"Load 'em in the boat. We'll take 'em to the cave."

"We haven't much time," Nick warned him.

"Don't worry," Stark said in a hard voice. "We're going to make quick work of 'em!"

CHAPTER XIX

Rocky Prison

FEAR showed in Jerry's eyes and his face paled. Joe stoically hid his emotions at Stark's ominous threat. The same thought raced wildly through the boys' minds. What would these men do to them?

While the two men forced Joe and Jerry into the brown boat, Frank was sending the *Sleuth* full speed toward Bayport harbor. Looking behind him, he frowned, puzzled.

"Where's the *Napoli*, Tony?" he asked. "Can you see it?"

Tony turned his head for a look. "No," he answered.

"They shouldn't be so far behind us," Frank said.

From time to time he glanced back uneasily, and as they sped across the bay toward the Coast

Guard station, he spoke up worriedly, "The *Napoli* isn't that much slower than the *Sleuth*. Maybe the boat had motor trouble."

"Don't think so," Tony said, tight-lipped. "Just had her checked."

Frank throttled down his engine as the *Sleuth* slid in beside the pier. Making a line fast to a pile, he leaped onto the ladder and climbed up.

"Take it easy, Tony. I'll get help," he said, and sprinted along the wharf to the Coast Guard headquarters.

"I have a fellow in my boat with an injured ankle," he told Lieutenant Parker breathlessly.

A few moments later four Coast Guardmen, two with a stretcher between them, were running with Frank to the end of the pier. Expertly, the rescue team carried Tony up the ladder and laid him on the stretcher.

"Okay, Tony?" Frank inquired.

"Sure," came the plucky reply. "You'd better forget me, Frank, and think about Joe and Jerry. Something must have happened to them!"

"We must get Tony to a doctor," Frank told Lieutenant Parker, as both hurried along beside the stretcher.

"Our men will take him," the young officer said. "We have an emergency vehicle ready at all times. But what was he talking about, Frank? Is something else wrong?"

"I'll tell you in a minute," the boy replied.

"We might need a cutter and some men soon. May I use your phone?"

Frank went into the Coast Guard station and called police headquarters.

"Chief Collig?" he began urgently. "This is Frank Hardy. I'm at the Coast Guard pier. Just got back from Hermit Island. We've found the jackets the bank robbers were wearing. I have two of them. Joe ought to be here with the others any minute."

"What!" Collig cried in amazement. "Stay there. I'll be right down," he said.

After hanging up, Frank dashed out of the station and ran to the end of the pier again. Frowning, he scanned the waters of the bay. He could not see the *Napoli*, and he returned to the station.

"Our men have taken Tony to a doctor," Lieutenant Parker told him. "Have you found some new clue to the bank robbers or your missing chums, Frank? If there's going to be trouble, we want to help."

Frank quickly gave details and ended with, "I'm worried about Joe and Jerry."

"What do you think happened to them?"

"I don't know. There was one member of the gang on the island when Tony and I left. Maybe more of them came back. The boys may have been trapped."

"I'll order the cutter at once," Lieutenant Parker said.

"Thanks," Frank replied. "If we don't see the *Napoli* by the time Chief Collig gets here, we'd better move fast!"

Nervously the boy paced about the pier with his eyes fixed on the harbor mouth. Still no *Napoli*. Frank heard a siren wail and a black police car sped up to the Coast Guard station.

"Joe hasn't come yet," he told the chief. "I'm afraid something went wrong out at the island."

"Then we'd better get there fast!" Collig snapped.

The powerful engines of a Coast Guard cutter were rumbling impatiently beside the pier. Frank, Chief Collig, and the two policemen he had brought along hurried aboard. Already a squad of seamen armed with rifles had taken their places. At a signal from Lieutenant Parker the cutter growled out into the bay.

On Hermit Island the two robbers had hauled Joe and Jerry along the path toward the cave. When they reached the entrance, they noted that the radio inside was still playing.

Stark's face tightened with anger. "Hold them here with your gun, Nick," he ordered, and disappeared into the cavern. The music stopped suddenly, and Stark came out a few moments later, pushing a heavy, bald-headed man, who blinked in the late-afternoon sunlight.

"It's the fellow we saw with Ben Stark in the *Black Cat!*" Joe thought.

He also noted that the man was wearing the same clothing the fake hermit had had on the day before. But this man was clean shaven and in his thirties! "He must have been wearing a false beard yesterday," Joe decided.

Fritz Stark glowered at the bald man. "Listen, Pops," he demanded, "how did these kids get on the island? You're supposed to be keeping people away—not sleeping!"

"Pops!" said Joe to himself. "This is the fellow Alf told us about who beat up Sutton!"

The bald man answered Stark lamely. "I guess I was in the cave and didn't hear them. I figured nobody would be nosing around during the storm."

"You fool!" Stark returned harshly. "These kids found three of our jackets—I saw them in their boat. What if they had made it to the police?"

"Well, we've got 'em now," Pops said.

"No thanks to you!" Nick put in angrily. "You're no good for anything but drinking soda and getting into fights!"

"Give him credit for buying postcards in Northport," Stark said sarcastically.

Pops bristled. "I did my share! We wouldn't

have stolen the crate of Yokohama radios so easy, if I hadn't first made the deal with Sutton."

"We'd have been better off without that hot-head," Nick declared.

"He knew the docks," Pops retorted. "Thanks to him we had inside help. If you guys hadn't been so slow we could've taken more crates."

"Oh, he was helpful," Stark sneered. "He wasn't satisfied with our bank loot. He brought the Hardys and the police down on our necks by planting a stolen radio on that big stevedore and making the whole bunch hot."

"And fighting with you over his cut every night in Shantytown. Did that help?" Nick asked sourly.

"You were all pretty careless," Joe egged them on. "We heard that an envelope from the Yoko-hama radio distributors was found in the Starks' hotel room."

Pops snorted in triumph. "You left that, Fritz!" he accused. "It was you who wrote pre-tending to be a purchasing agent to find out where their Super-X radio shipments came in."

"But Pops left his broken soda bottle in the *Sleuth*," Joe prodded.

"That's enough!" the bald man ordered. Roughly he shoved the captives toward the gap-ing cavern.

"Hold it!" Stark rasped. "First I have a bone to pick with this nosy kid." Then he cuffed Joe on the ear and laughed wickedly.

"What was that for?" Joe complained, trying to draw the man out more.

"You'd like to know, wouldn't you?" Stark sneered and pushed Joe so hard that he fell to the ground.

"Cut it out!" Jerry protested, and lunged forward to help his friend. Nick seized the boy and held him fast.

Stark yanked Joe up by the shoulders and yelled at him, "You and your pesky brother—always interfering with our plans! I had things all worked out!"

"I'll bet you did," Joe retorted. "Who stole the car in Northport?"

"Nick did," Stark replied, "while Ben and Pops took the *Black Cat* for a spin. Ben found out where your boat was kept, and later Pops took it."

"He broke into our boathouse while the rest of your gang was robbing the bank," Joe egged him on.

"That's right, smart boy." Fritz Stark sneered. "Ben was with us. Pops had the *Sleuth* waiting. We were going to head straight for Hermit Island."

Despite their predicament, Joe and Jerry could not help but gloat. "Instead, you landed high and dry miles up the coast," Joe said.

Stark's face darkened. "Yeah. Well, that didn't

stop us. We hotfooted it back to Shantytown, picked up Ben's car there, and drove around looking for another fast boat. We found one and 'borrowed' it."

"Ben ran the boat up the coast to Shantytown while I drove back. I'd heard over the radio your father was working on the bank robbery case. Soon as Ben got back to Shantytown, I told him about it and that I'd seen you Hardys in the costume store."

"So," Nick broke in, "Ben got the idea of kidnaping you two to make your old man drop the case."

"We told him what costume your brother was wearing," Fritz went on.

"And he sent two bunglers to do the job," Nick interrupted resentfully. "Moran and Duke! They drove to French's place and made him tell where the party was. Then they nabbed the wrong boys!"

"Where are they now?" Joe demanded. For answer their captors merely laughed.

"When did you discover who they were?" Joe asked. "After you took them to Shantytown?"

Stark shot him a hard look. "You know that, too?"

"Whoever tried to burn the costumes and hid the robbery masks didn't do a very good job," the young sleuth commented. "They were found."

"Duke's carelessness again," Pops muttered.

Nick cut in. "You fellows won't ever find your two friends. And nobody will find you!"

The boys learned the crooks had spotted the *Sleuth* and pretended to ram her to find out her full power. "We needed a fast boat for our get-away," Stark said, "and we knew yours would do."

Joe now said, "We saw you leaving the island during the storm. Why?"

Stark smiled briefly. "Nick and I had urgent business to check on in Bayport and no time to lose! We've got one more job to do tonight and then we're clearing out."

"And we need a fast boat to pull it," Pops said.

"You mean you'll leave your own brother in jail!" Joe taunted Stark. "You're a real pal!"

The man's face twitched with rage. "Listen, kid, I don't leave my brother in the lurch." He turned to Pops and snarled, "Get these guys in the cave! We'll take care of 'em later!"

The thug reinforced the belt which held Joe's hands with stout Manila rope. He tied Joe's ankles too, and then moved on to bind Jerry. All the while Joe thought over what he had learned. "Stark says they're doing one more job, and he won't abandon his brother. That must mean they went to Bayport to plan a jail break, which they're going to pull tonight. Then they'll all flee together!"

"All right—inside!" Pops ordered gruffly.

Stumbling in the gloom, Joe and Jerry were dragged far back into the cave. The place smelled musty and damp.

Stark threw them to the ground and walked away.

The boys waited in silence until their eyes became more accustomed to the darkness. Then Joe felt a chill up and down his spine as he discerned the shape of someone lying beside him! Could it be Chet or Biff?

Wriggling over, Joe nudged the unknown prisoner. He moaned, as though dazed, and turned his face upward.

"Jumping catfish!" Joe whispered hoarsely. "It's Mr. French!"

CHAPTER XX

Ambushing the Enemy

"MR. FRENCH, what happened?" Joe asked in amazement.

Painfully the costume dealer drew himself to a sitting position. "It was terrible," he answered shakily. "Where am I? I was blindfolded by the men who brought me here."

"You're in a cave on Hermit Island," Joe told him. "How are you mixed up in this, Mr. French? I wondered once if you belonged to the gang."

"*No!*" the man protested. "You must believe me, boy. The mental anguish I've gone through since I sold those men the masks for the robbery! I neglected my business entirely—didn't even check my stock.

"Fritz Stark and Nick Glaser were in the shop when you stopped in for your costumes that afternoon. They had come to pick up the masks they'd ordered. I asked if they were going to a party.

Glaser laughed and said, 'Yes—a big surprise party!' When I went in the back to get the masks, I heard them laugh again and mention the bank."

"So you put two and two together," Jerry said.

"That's right. I guessed they were crooks."

"You should have tipped us off," Joe said. "Why didn't you go to the police?"

Mr. French said brokenly, "I had made the mistake of telling them my suspicions and who you were. They said they'd kill me and harm my family if I talked. I sent my family away for safety."

"Why did you come to our house that night?" Joe asked sympathetically.

"The other morning they began to use my store as one of their meeting places and told me to give my assistant a short vacation. I heard them bragging they were going to kidnap you and your brother. Later something snapped inside me. Robbery is bad enough, but I couldn't let them get away with kidnaping no matter what they did to me. So I went to tell your father everything."

"But Frank and I answered the door," Joe prompted.

"Yes," French agreed. "When I saw you were safe, it confused me. Besides, I had a strange feeling I was being followed. I didn't know what to do, so I came away without telling my story."

"What happened then?" Joe asked.

"Well, when Fritz Stark and Nick Glaser came to the shop early yesterday afternoon, I got my nerve back and told them I'd spill everything if they didn't let me alone."

"What did they do?" Jerry asked.

"Stark said they'd let me alone if I'd do two things for them. First he made me put the gorilla and the magician suits in the window. They were a signal to the rest of the thieves to knock three times at the back door. The gang was going to have a meeting about something."

Joe laughed grimly. "Yes, to plan to kidnap Frank and me. I guess that's why they used our costumes in the window."

"There was only one costume—a skeleton suit —on display this morning," Jerry remembered.

"Fritz Stark put it there last night. He took my key. I overheard him say a single costume meant 'Danger. Stay away,' " French explained.

"Stark put up the warning signal too late. He didn't know then that half the gang was in jail."

"That's right," the man said. "It was after he left the skeleton warning that he found out Ben and the others were captured."

"I'll bet the second thing they wanted you to do, Mr. French, was to sell three radios to the hi-fi shop," Joe guessed.

"Yes," said the man, surprised, "and immediately. Glaser walked down to the shop with me and waited on the sidewalk. As I came out, Stark drove up in their car, forced me to get in, and blindfolded me. The last thing I remember before I came to in this cave was trying to break loose and jump out."

"They must have slugged you," Joe said.

"But what good will it do you to know all this?" Mr. French said despairingly. "We'll never get out of here alive. These men mean business!"

"So do we," Joe promised grimly. In rapid whispers he told the despondent man how he and Frank, by offering themselves as bait, had trapped Ben Stark and his two henchmen. "But we haven't been able to find Chet and Biff. Do you know where they are?"

The costume dealer shook his head helplessly. "No. You can see for yourself they're not in here. I wanted to look for the stolen money, but naturally I didn't dare. This is the end for us, I'm afraid."

Joe tried to reassure him. "My brother is free. When Jerry and I fail to show up, he'll bring help."

"I only hope he's in time," said Mr. French. "I heard these men planning to leave here in a little while. They said they'd dispose of me before they push off."

Jerry looked grimly at Joe. "That goes for us too, I guess!"

As dusk fell, the prisoners waited anxiously. While Joe tried to keep Mr. French's spirits up, Jerry watched Stark and Pops passing and repassing before the entrance.

"Joe," he said after a while, "I haven't seen those two guys outside for the last ten minutes. Do you think something's up?"

The three prisoners stiffened, all senses alert.

"Sh!" Joe hissed suddenly. "Listen!" In the distance they heard a motorboat.

"That's a big one," Jerry whispered excitedly. "Sounds like a cutter."

"It's coming here!" Joe said as the sound grew louder. Suddenly it ceased and they heard shouts in the distance, then closer.

"It's Frank!" Joe exclaimed. "Sing out, everybody!"

"Halloo! Frank! Help! In here!"

Their voices rang and echoed hollowly against the rock walls. Before long, the beam of a flashlight pierced the cave opening.

"Joe! Jerry!" came an anxious, familiar voice. "You okay?"

"Back here, Frank!" Joe called eagerly to his brother.

Seconds later, Frank and two young Coast Guardmen were cutting the ropes that bound the prisoners.

"Mr. French!" cried Frank in recognition. "So the gang had you, too! Are Chet and Biff here?"

"No!" his brother replied worriedly. "And neither are the bank robbers."

Already the cave was filled with men. Flashlight beams flickered up and down the damp walls. Seamen and policemen stood by with guns ready. Chief Collig and Lieutenant Parker hurried into the cave.

"You boys all right?" he demanded.

"We're okay," Joe answered, "but we must go after the robbers. Two of them—Fritz Stark and Pops—were here twenty minutes ago. And Nick Glaser, who drove the getaway car, was here too."

"They probably spotted the cutter and headed for their boat or the *Napoli*," said Joe.

Quickly he described the location of the hidden inlet where the *Napoli* and the robbers' stolen craft were concealed. Lieutenant Parker immediately dispatched men to the spot.

"With a twenty-minute head start," Joe said, "Fritz Stark and the other two probably will get away."

"But the cutter could pick them up easily," Jerry put in.

"Right," said Frank. "Those men know they haven't a chance against the Coast Guard. I think they're hiding here."

"Where?" asked Mr. French.

"We'll comb the island," Lieutenant Parker said.

"Let's search this cave first," Frank suggested. "There's a slight draft coming from the back. That might mean there's another chamber." Slowly Frank played the beam of his flashlight over the rear wall until he spotted a narrow crevice. He stepped quickly over and shone his beam into it.

"Look!" he exclaimed softly.

Joe, Chief Collig, and Lieutenant Parker crowded around. In front of them, well inside the opening, hung a piece of burlap. Frank slipped into the crevice and pulled the rough curtain aside. A long rock passage was revealed.

"Come on!" Joe exclaimed. "Let's go!"

As Joe stepped forward, Chief Collig clamped a hand on his shoulder. "Hold it," the chief ordered. "Let the armed men go first. Those crooks are desperate and won't hesitate to use their guns." Reluctantly, all three boys heeded the order.

At Collig's signal, Parker drew his service revolver and led the men into the narrow rock corridor. The chief and his two policemen followed, with Frank, Joe, and Jerry impatiently bringing up the rear.

The narrow passage twisted and turned. Only one kind of sound could be heard—the heavy breathing of the pursuers. Suddenly there came an earsplitting *crack!* A gunshot from up front!

"Halt!" Lieutenant Parker's voice rang out. "Do *not* return fire!"

The file of men flattened against the rocks. The boys craned to see what was happening.

In a chamber at the end of the passage, their hands tied, stood Chet and Biff! Behind them were Stark and Pops, a cloud of gun smoke above them.

Though the two men were using the captives as shields, and the situation was desperate, Frank, Joe, and Jerry were jubilant. They had found their missing chums!

The Coast Guardmen and the police were forced to stand by helplessly, not daring to endanger Chet and Biff. But Joe saw a chance to change the situation. At a signal, he motioned Frank and Jerry to back out of the passage quietly. The three dashed from the cave.

"Stark and Pops got in there, somehow," Joe said. "They didn't come past us. There must be another entrance out here."

Hastily, in the gathering twilight, the boys examined the irregular face of the bluff. Suddenly Frank pointed to a big dark crack in the rock. As they neared it, a man's figure loomed in the opening.

Without hesitation the three boys hurled themselves on the man and bore him to the ground. He hit with a thud, the fight knocked out of him.

"It's Nick Glaser," Joe whispered as Jerry whipped off the man's belt and bound his arms securely with it.

"Okay," Jerry replied, "I'll watch him. Don't worry, he won't get away."

The Hardys slipped into the dark crack from

which the man had emerged. Snapping out his flashlight, Frank groped forward as fast as he dared. Soon he could make out the yellow glare of the rescuers' flashlights, and the backs of Pops and Fritz Stark, standing behind Biff and Chet!

"For the last time, I tell you throw down your guns," Stark ordered, "if you don't want these kids hurt!"

Without pausing, Frank and Joe charged forward. Together they let drive with two bruising tackles. The legs of the criminals buckled underneath them. The revolvers flew from their hands and the men landed, dazed, on the floor of the cave. The police and seamen were upon them in a second.

"Frank! Joe!" cried Chet, overjoyed. As soon as his hands were untied, the stout boy grabbed his pals and hugged them in his excitement.

"O-of! Hey, don't crush us!" Joe protested, laughing.

"We thought you'd never find us in this place!" Biff put in, rubbing his chafed wrists.

"We were plenty worried ourselves," Frank admitted.

"They took us to Shantytown first in Stark's car." Chet spilled out the story. "Were they mad when they found out we weren't you and Joe!"

"But they were afraid to let us go," Biff went on, "so they took away our costumes and brought us here in a small boat."

"On the way, they threw our masks overboard," Chet said, "hoping you'd think we drowned."

"We found yours," Frank told him.

"Because it was made of rubber," Biff put in. "Mine was only paper, so it was lost."

"And the day we got here, Pops went for the postcards," Chet continued. "Fritz Stark dictated what we had to write."

"We told them you wouldn't be fooled," Biff added, "but Pops took the cards back to Northport and mailed 'em, anyhow."

"We found out a lot," Chet continued. "This outfit is part of a national ring of bank robbers. Duke, Moran, and Glaser were sent first to 'case' the banks around here and decided on Bayport."

"Do you know where the loot is?" Joe asked.

"Right here, I'll bet!" Chet pointed at his feet. "I noticed loose earth the first day."

Immediately Frank and Joe, aided by the two policemen, began to scoop away the earth with pocketknives and their bare hands. In a few minutes they had dragged out the canvas sacks filled with money!

"Now, one more thing," Joe said. "Let's search for the rest of the Yokohama radios."

"They're right over here," Biff volunteered, and led the others to a shadowy corner of the cave where an opened crate stood. "Chet and I have been tied up next to them all the time. Those crooks were sure mad at Sutton—said it was his fault they only dared sell three."

"Jerry has the last member of the gang outside, Chief Collig," Frank concluded. "Once you handcuff him, we can all go back home."

Lieutenant Parker said he would take charge of the stolen boat and return the craft to its owner. A seaman was assigned to bring in the *Napoli*.

The evening shadows were lengthening as the rest of the party boarded the cutter. First of all, Frank told Jerry and Joe about Tony. They were relieved he had not been seriously injured. By the time the boat entered the wide mouth of the bay, the harbor lights were twinkling.

News of the capture had been radioed ahead, so the Morton and Hooper families were on the pier to embrace their sons. Fenton Hardy, too, came forward to congratulate Frank and Joe and their chums.

"A fine job," he said. "And you'll be glad to hear," he went on, "that the bank robbery ring has been put out of business nationally as well as locally. The leader's arrest this afternoon at a secret hideout in California clinched matters."

A cheer arose from the whole group. Nodding modestly, Mr. Hardy explained, "The robbers we rounded up here talked, hoping for clemency, so that made the job simple."

When Mr. Hardy finished speaking, Collig boomed out, "I congratulate you, boys. You solved three mysteries at once. And you even helped us round up two crooked dockmen."

For a moment the Hardys were silent, wondering how soon another case might come their way. They were to find out in the near future while *Hunting for Hidden Gold.*

"There's one question I'd like to have answered," Joe said, coming back to the present. "Who were Stark and Moran waiting for on the pier the night Dad trailed them?"

"For Pops," Lieutenant Daley replied. "He was supposed to meet them there in a small boat and help pull off another theft—this time valuable radios from Germany."

Pat Muster chortled. "But the weather was uncertain and the big, bold bandit said he was afraid to make the trip!"

Frank spoke up. "One last question. Why was Pops called Pops, anyhow?"

"Because he drinks soda pop all the time," replied Chet. "His favorite is some stuff named Fizzle."

"I wonder," said Joe with a grin, "if he'll be served any Fizzle in jail!"

Match Wits with The Hardy Boys®!

Collect the Complete
Hardy Boys Mystery Stories®
by Franklin W. Dixon

The Hardy Boys Back-to-Back
#1: The Tower Treasure/#2: The House on the Cliff

Celebrate over 70 Years with the World's Greatest Super Sleuths!

Match Wits with Super Sleuth Nancy Drew!

Collect the Complete
Nancy Drew Mystery Stories®
by Carolyn Keene

Celebrate over 70 years with the World's Best Detective!

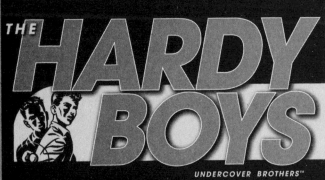